ELIZABETH COLE

SUSAN CHEEVER

Farrar Straus Giroux

New York

ELIZABETH COLE

Library of Congress Cataloging-in-Publication Data
Cheever, Susan.
Elizabeth Cole
p.   cm.
I. Title.
PS3553.H3487E45   1989
813'.54—dc20   89-1499

for David Rieff

ELIZABETH COLE

1 My name is Elizabeth Cole. I'm thirty years old, and I'm in love with a married man. I grew up in New Haven, Connecticut, in a family where mixing a martini was the popular sport and backgammon the accepted form of gambling. Our dogs were treated like royalty, and when my younger brother and I misbehaved, we were sometimes swatted with a rolled-up newspaper.

Cole is a name we were told was brought from England by my great-grandfather Aaron Cole, an abolitionist who emigrated to join the Union Army; it's a name my father has made moderately famous as a painter. My mother chose Elizabeth because she was pleased by the possibility of all the cute Elizabeth nicknames: Betsy, Beth, Muffy, Liz, and Libby. As it turns out, almost everyone calls me Elizabeth.

After high school in New Haven, we children were duly shipped off to college: my brother to Berkeley, because it was thought he should sow his wild oats on another coast before settling down in some appropriate profession like medicine or the law, and me to the Ivy League, because my father thought I should be exposed to scholarly influences before embarking on my career as a woman—by which he meant finding the right husband and dabbling charmingly in the arts. Instead I moved to Greenwich Village and got a job on a magazine. A year ago, I met Sebastian.

As I wait for him to walk from one of the TWA jetways at Kennedy Airport, I wonder what it would be like if *we* were married. Wives don't stand expectantly, with their heart rates accelerating, waiting for their husbands to get off airplanes— I know that much. It's early morning and the sun, still concealed behind the edge of the world, glints below the horizon of Far Rockaway and flashes on the wings of the big jets. The planes are clumsy, creaking conglomerations of metal and plastic, but from behind the glass of the terminal windows they're like enormous, silent birds leaping into the air with unnatural force. Suddenly, out of the crowd I see Sebastian coming toward me.

"Hi, pretty girl," he says, leaning over to kiss me. He smells of diesel fuel, bad coffee, and his sandalwood after-shave lotion. Even the day-old stubble on his jaw seems a cultivated allusion to the roughness of manhood, the dangers of travel.

"Good trip?" I ask. I want to grab him in a jubilant embrace and press him against the white walls of the terminal. I restrain myself. Sebastian doesn't approve of public display.

"The usual. Late taking off, circling over Pittsburgh. It's good to see you." He gives my shoulder a squeeze with his free hand, the other holds his leather garment bag and his briefcase, filled with slides of the paintings he buys and sells.

"Did you get any sleep? Did you dream about me?"

"You know I dream about you whether I sleep or not."

I take his arm as we descend the broad steps toward the parking lot. There's a regal quality to Saarinen's architecture which suggests a high-school band playing "Pomp and Circumstance" for graduation.

"Come here," he says when we reach the car, and he hugs me hard at last, pressing me against his chest as if he wanted to glue us together. It would be all right with me.

"I missed you so much," I say, but Sebastian draws back and opens the door of the car, throwing his gleaming black leather bag on the battered narrow back seat, which is strewn with old galleys and pasteup boards from the magazine where I work. I inherited the Red Menace—a faded ten-year-old convertible—from my brother, Andrew, the last time he announced his engagement to Karen and she persuaded him to buy a grown-up car, a car more appropriate to his standing as a fast-track uptown lawyer. The engagement lasted only a month that time, but the Red Menace is mine and Andrew is stuck with a silver two-door that gets broken into every time he parks it on the street.

When he's feeling rich, my father sometimes offers to buy me a new car, and I tell him I don't need one. I know it wouldn't be a convertible, and it probably wouldn't be red.

"I missed *you*," Sebastian answers over the car's patched gray top.

"It's easier to be the one who leaves."

"I don't know. Is missing a competitive sport?"

"I'm training for the next Olympics," I say. He settles into the passenger seat. I like having him captive in my little car, which putts along out of the airport and then begins its habitual, even growl as I ease onto the Van Wyck Expressway toward the city.

"I love to watch you drive, you're so fierce about it," Sebastian says as I pass a blue stretch limo with three huge aerials and scoot out onto Grand Central Parkway.

"I am fierce," I say. "I'm an animal!" They can have their limos.

"You're an animal. What type?" He reaches out across the emergency brake and the stick shift and strokes my thigh. "Should I be frightened?"

"Very." I lean toward him as I drive.

"The hell of it is that because the plane was late I have to get right home. There's a call I have to make"—he glances at his watch—"about now."

"At eight o'clock in the morning?"

"To Japan," he says.

"Oh, right." This reminder of Sebastian's other life—his work and his Park Avenue wife and children—unsettles me. He takes his hand off my leg and turns to extract his briefcase from the back seat. I change lanes and pass a maroon car on the right.

"This car makes me nervous," Sebastian says, fiddling with the brass latches on the briefcase.

"This car is great," I say. "There were times when this car

was my best friend." I slow down as we pass Hoyt Avenue, cars are piling up on the approach to the Triborough Bridge.

"Can it go any faster?" Sebastian looks at his watch again. His cuff links flash.

"Maybe you should have taken a cab," I say, "or a limo; then the driver wouldn't mind being told what to do."

"Don't be so sensitive. It's just that when you're talking you drive so slowly. Can't you understand that I'm worried about time?"

"Right, and you're the only person in the world who has anything to do or anywhere to go. These other cars have some nerve, slowing you down like this!"

"All I'm asking is that you pay attention when you drive."

"I was paying attention to something else, *excuse* me."

"Okay." Sebastian looks out the window away from me as we cross the bridge. I throw a token into the plastic basket at the tollbooth in silence.

"I'm glad to see you?" Sebastian says.

"Fuck you," I say.

"Elizabeth, let's not fight. I *am* glad to see you. I'm sorry if I was cross."

"I'm nice enough to pick you up at the airport at dawn, *I'm* going to be late for work, and you're treating me like a servant!"

"I give up! You're right, I'm an unfeeling rat."

My outburst has made Sebastian laugh. "Jesus, Elizabeth, how do you put up with me? How are you ever going to put up with me?" His hand is on my thigh again and he reaches over to push my shoulder against his.

"There are compensations," I say grudgingly, but I'm laughing, too. "Stop that!" He's pushing me against the door; I pull the steering wheel to keep my balance and the car veers to the right.

"There's only one way to make me stop," he says. "Otherwise . . . death on the FDR Drive."

"You'll really be late! What about your important phone call, your Japanese collector?"

"Fuck my Japanese collector," he says.

"I'd be jealous. Is he cute?"

"I missed you, I need you to keep me from misbehaving."

"I thought you wanted to misbehave."

"Yes, please."

"All right." I assume the tone of a scolding nanny. "Just this once; but don't blame me if you're late for everything."

"Just this once?"

"A special treat," I say. Downtown on Sullivan Street there's nowhere to park. Alternate-side-of-the-street parking regulations have cleared one side for the street cleaner and I pull up illegally in front of the town house where I live in a top-floor apartment. We leave his bag and briefcase in the car and hurry upstairs. Sebastian presses against me, discovering my familiar body with his hands as I unlock the door.

Inside, I slip off my blazer and press Sebastian to the wall next to the couch, reaching up to kiss his face and neck, and reaching down. He moves toward the bedroom.

"No, I can't wait," I say, pulling him toward the couch, pushing him down so that he's sitting.

"You can't wait." He smiles as I stand above him pulling off my jeans. "Such impatience!" But his voice is low and rough.

Later we walk, holding hands, back to the car. There's no ticket, and Sebastian's bag and briefcase are still there on the cluttered back seat. The world is ours.

"I'll give you a lift uptown," I say. We're both bathed in a luminescent glow of mellow pride and pleasure. We couldn't wait, the bedroom was too far. My times with Sebastian, I think, are as precious as jewels, diamonds and rubies and emeralds, amethyst and citrine, piles of them shimmering in some golden fairy tale. Love is the most powerful drug in the world, a potent fluid that drops slowly into my veins as Sebastian and I make love. It's a drug I crave, a drug I have to have, a drug that yields moments of serenity that I don't find anywhere else in my life. There are times, lying next to Sebastian after we make love, when I feel completely in harmony with my body and with his, with my apartment and the whole city and the world and the planets spinning with it around the sun. This is where I am meant to be, I think then. This is my place.

"I can take a cab," he says. I see the erosion of everyday life on Sebastian's face. He's remembering the crises at his art gallery, the call to Japan he didn't make, all the things he has to do today, his job as executor of the painter George Mallet's estate, his children's expectations, all the things he should have been doing in the two hours since his plane landed.

"Get in," I say. Obediently, because it's easier and probably faster, he gets in the car, but he opens his briefcase on his lap as I turn up Sixth Avenue. A look at his apointment book makes him groan, and when we get caught in the morning traffic around the garment district, his knee bounces nervously against the dashboard in the cramped front seat.

"I should have just gone straight to the gallery," he says as I cut into the park at Central Park South, narrowly missing a horse-drawn carriage clip-clopping down Fifty-ninth Street. Then we're both silent. I pull up outside Sebastian's building on the east side of Park Avenue. The doorman hesitates at the sight of my car, but then, recognizing Sebastian, he comes to open the door. Sebastian reaches over as the doorman waits and gives me a perfunctory kiss, as if I were just some kid he happened to hitch a ride with. An hour ago he was grunting in my arms!

"Let's get away for a weekend soon," he says to me in a lowered voice.

"Good idea," I say, to show him that I'm not annoyed . . . much. He steps out of the car and hands the elderly, blue-and-gold-liveried doorman the bag he carried so easily through the airport. It's as if the Sebastian I know is a younger, stronger man than this Mr. Smith whose bag is being carried for him by someone who looks old enough to be his father.

"I'll call you this afternoon," he says as he shuts the car door. The doorman is watching. I wait as Sebastian is ushered like Little Lord Fauntleroy into the splendid marble, mahogany, and brass lobby of his building. When he disappears, and

the huge wrought-iron doors swing shut behind him, I step
on the gas and U-turn illegally around the traffic island on
Park, headed downtown toward work. At the next light, I turn
on the radio and let it blare. It's "Will You Love Me Tomorrow," and I sing along with The Shirelles. I know Sebastian
would be horrified if he saw me now, chewing gum, driving
like a kid, and braying a golden oldie.

2   Through my bedroom door I can see dim outlines of the furniture in the living room where streetlights cast crazy patterns against the ceiling in the dark. I think I hear a sound out there, a footstep or a drawer opening. Quickly, before I have a chance to panic, I walk through the door and turn on the lights. There's nothing there, no one, but now I wonder if the noise I heard came from outside in the hall or down on the landing.

In the morning, the fears are gone. I make coffee and open my door for the newspaper without even looking down the stairs. Then I shower, put on black pants and a shirt with big shoulder pads and head downtown to the magazine offices— two huge rooms in an old thread factory dominated by Judith Grimes-Gurewitz's massive, ugly, Italian-design desk.

A year ago *Antics* was bought by pet-food tycoon Philip Goff from the group of editors who had put it together. Since then, the friends I had there have left. The Grimy Guru, who used to wear post-hippie long skirts and shawls and who worked day and night, now wears little blue-and-gray success suits and spends most of her time going uptown for lunches or executive meetings. The new editor is a former public-affairs genius, and the people he hired to replace our motley but spirited staff are either lackadaisical drones or professionally restless types who talk all the time about the Great Creative careers they will have when they break free from the bonds of salaried journalism. Their glorious talents are temporarily held in check by rude economic necessity. These people make me happy that I've decided never to be a painter like my rich friend Ingrid, or my father, the great Fairfax Cole.

In the meantime, the art department has disintegrated, and I'm doing more work and different kinds of work. That, and | 11 my own rude economic necessities, are what keep me here. I've begun doing drawings and design as well as layouts— there's often no one else who knows how.

"You're more interesting than anything you do," Sebastian says. I'm flattered and I'm resentful, because he's right. It doesn't seem to bother *him*.

The past seems immeasurably distant now, like someone else's story, but it was less than a year ago that Sebastian and I went up to New Hampshire to mountain climb—our first weekend away together. Until that weekend I had been telling him that he shouldn't be cheating on his wife. And he had been telling me that his marriage was basically solid. Until then I still spent a lot of time thinking about Casey and the ways things had gone wrong between us. I wondered what Casey would think if he heard that I had landed a wealthy art dealer, the famous Sebastian Smith. Sebastian didn't ask me to take risks and chances that scared me; with him everything was convenient and arranged in advance. In New Hampshire we stayed at a cozy inn near the mountains. If anything, it was me who was willing to take chances and Sebastian who hung back.

The weather was marvelous that weekend, the air smelled of cider and pine woods. It was hot for November, and as we climbed I took off my down vest and then my sweater. Clambering past the last cairns, we emerged suddenly at the summit, standing together in the middle of the still blue autumn sky. Clouds to the west over the Connecticut Valley piled up into great cumulus anvils with rays of the sun streaming through them onto the state's tapestry of silver lakes. Northeast, toward the snow-covered peaks of the Presidential Range, fleecy cirri scudded toward Pinkham Notch, where there was a line of overcast sky above the horizon and the mountains shaded from brown to black. It was as if we could see the whole world.

The climb down was hotter; clouds gathered above the pines and the air was broody and humid as if a storm was blowing in. When we got to the place where Eagle Brook crosses the Greenleaf Trail we sat down on a carpet of moss next to the water. There was snow in the woods from early storms, but the granite was warm and the sun turned the brook to gold as it cascaded down into the potholes below where we sat.

I stood up and stripped off my shirt and bra and undid my pants.

"Elizabeth, what on earth are you doing?"

"I'm hot, aren't you hot? Come on!"

"You're crazy, it's the middle of winter, the water's freezing. What if someone comes?"

"They'll have a nice surprise." His caution turned me on; now I had to do it. My heart seemed to stop as I slid down the smooth rock surface into the stream, past shining flakes of mica imbedded in the schist. The water felt as pure as stone, as cold as ice against my skin.

"Come on in, it feels great. *Very* refreshing!" I gasped. My nerves shrieked and tingled, my blood raced, and I smiled invitingly from the water. Sebastian demurred. He rolled up his chinos and put one foot in.

"Jesus," he said. "Forget it."

"It feels colder if you do it that way, you just have to commit yourself all at once."

"Not a chance," Sebastian said. I climbed out onto the bank and felt the rush of energy and relief that warm air brings.

"Too old for this, huh?" I teased. It felt wonderful to be out of the water, wonderful to be alive and warm again. He stepped toward me and wrapped his soft blue sweater around my shivering, dripping shoulders.

"No, just too sane," he said. "You're nuts, Elizabeth, you need someone to protect you from your own impulses." There was respect in his voice, though, respect and lust. "Your skin is icy." He stroked my back with his warm hands.

"And you're so warm." I trembled, naked against him. He pressed me close, pushing down the sweater. "Are you too sane to fuck me?"

"Right here?" But Sebastian was turned on, too. The exhilaration of the day, the risks of making love on a public trail had gotten to him.

"No, over there, on the moss." I drew him toward the flattest, softest part of the rock, where we had been sitting earlier. He made a pillow out of his sweater.

It was after that that I began to daydream about Sebastian all the time. Somehow that moment on Mount Lafayette infected me with a longing for him and I caught myself thinking about what it would be like to live with him. I listened to his complaints about his wife with a sharper ear.

Sunday night we drove back to the city. He had told Melissa he was in Boston on business, and as we crossed the Massachusetts Turnpike at Sturbridge we laughed at her for believing him. At dinnertime, Sebastian remembered a little restaurant off the Tolland exit of the Wilbur Cross.

"Is there anywhere in the world you don't know of a little place to eat?" I asked after the owner had made a fuss over Sebastian and he had ordered for both of us. Sebastian was completely at home and in command everywhere.

"I like to be comfortable." He shrugged off the question. "Don't you think this corn chowder is good?"

"The whole place isn't bad." We sat in a dark wooden booth opposite a fire which lit the rest of the old tavern.

"Maybe too much cream," Sebastian said. "It should be a little lighter."

"Most people don't take their food so seriously. They just stop at McDonald's or whatever." When my family traveled, we always stopped in the restaurants where the bartender made the strongest drinks. My father measured both character and comfort by this standard. A man who made weak drinks was a sissy. A real man, he used to say, could make a martini strong enough to draw a boat.

Sebastian made a face, as if the thought of McFood and its cardboard hamburgers and plastic shakes was a personal offense. "Why live at all if you don't do it right?" he said.

"Living well is the best revenge?" I sounded sarcastic, but I was envious.

"You're making too much of this." Sebastian tasted his veal marsala and gave the waiter an approving nod.

"No, I really mean it."

"I don't have your freedom, you know that."

"But I'm a wreck, I need someone to protect me from my own impulses," I said. "Look at what you have; you wouldn't give up what you have."

"Try me," he said.

"Come on. Great work you love, a good family, time to go off on sexy weekends with young things who adore you!"

"Elizabeth!" Sebastian reached for my hand across the tablecloth, past the loaf of bread. "Don't tease me."

"Well, Sebastiaaaan"—I drew his name out like a chant—"isn't that the truth?"

"Has it occurred to you that I'm falling in love with you?" he said.

I laughed and my heart did a secret jig. "Maybe you need someone to protect you from *your* impulses," I said.

"Please stop." Sebastian had put down his fork.

"Of course you're in love with me. I'm the elusive one, the unattainable. I'm what you can't have, so you can't get enough right now. You were probably in love with Melissa once."

"No, not like this." He poured us both more wine and I noticed the bottle was empty.

"Sex has turned your head," I said, "you're not thinking straight." Whatever Sebastian gave me made me want more. If he made love to me, I wanted him to love me. If he said he loved me, I wanted him to leave his wife and marry me. I was floundering, why shouldn't he flounder, too? But my friend Julie's coaching had taught me never to let my needs show. Catching a man was like taming a wild animal: you laid a fine net along the leaves and brush on the forest floor and waited. I heard the first footfall in the distance, the snap of a twig and the crunch of leaves underfoot.

"Remember"—Julie was sitting up in bed drinking Calvados from a big snifter. A paperback of *Thérèse* lay face down against the pale green quilt. "Remember that men always do exactly what you ask them *not* to do. It's the Br'er Rabbit and Br'er Fox principle of heterosexual relations."

Julie lives with her daughter Samantha in a brownstone on my block. I usually stop there at least once a day for advice. Julie always has advice.

After that dinner with Sebastian I drove south on the noisy concrete sections of the turnpike, and he fell asleep next to me in the leather seat of his own car. I guided the perfectly tuned machine through the night, past New Haven and Bridge-port and toward the city, as he breathed trustingly next to me, his life in my hands, the great Sebastian Smith snoozing like a kid. His hair was rumpled into a cowlick and his cheek dented by the seams of the seat. As we crossed the bridge into Manhattan, he woke up and shifted his body toward me.

"Oh, Elizabeth, my delight," he said as I turned south on the FDR Drive. "I'll miss you so much." I stroked his head as if he were a child, consoling him for our imminent sepa-ration, consoling him for my lonely nights.

3 "Why did you fall in love with a married man?" Dr. Rosen asks. It's a recurrent question in our weekly fifty-minute hours. Sometimes it makes me cry. My answers are not psychiatrically satisfactory.

"I love him," I say, weeping. "Does there have to be a reason?" As I cry, Dr. Rosen leans slightly forward. An empty paper coffee cup from the deli tilts on the desk behind him. He turns in his leather chair and presses the tips of his fingers together to make a steeple.

"If you're still acting out a childhood experience," he says, "you'll always be competing with another woman."

"I don't mind competing with Melissa." My crying has stopped. "What I mind is that she's winning." Behind him I watch autumn rain falling on the flat tar roofs and wooden water towers of the Upper East Side.

"A married man is not really available," he says. "You can't get to know him, there's no possibility of building a life together."

"Maybe I'm attracted to his life." The black-tie dinners, the glamorous collectors, and the trips to Europe. I have one short black evening dress. Melissa's closet is a cloud of colored taffeta and silk. "The truth is that it's not so bad being a mistress. It's fun! Every moment counts."

"But they're moments!"

"I'd trade a boring year for a thrilling moment. Marriage is all that dailiness; doing the dishes, and how was your day, dear, and did you remember to pay the Con Ed bill. In an affair . . ."

"But life is a daily proposition, Elizabeth." Dr. Rosen's eyelids are drooping. When I talk about myself he looks tired.

For a moment I hate him. He's probably been married forever to someone awful—and I'm glad. "What you're talking about leads nowhere."

"Men leave their wives," I say.

"But it can be serious only when it changes, when the illicit excitement is gone and you're not a bad little girl anymore." Dr. Herbert Rosen, M.D., whose strict Freudian principles prohibit any revelation of his address, his personal history, or his state of mind, lets his long face reveal his opinion of my Great Love.

As I leave his office and walk over to Fifth Avenue, I pass a thin woman with streaked blond hair, pressed blue jeans, and a green monogrammed sweater. They're all Melissas here on the Upper East Side, with their perfect little features and their designer sports clothes and their towheaded toddlers. Buildings full of Melissas, stores for Melissas, a whole neighborhood of Melissas! I step on the bus and sit looking out at the park.

"I want to show you something," Sebastian says later, after dinner. He pours more champagne from the black-and-gold bottle on the table in the back room of his gallery.

"Have you ever made love back here?" I say. It's late, and Sebastian has let us into the empty building with his keys.

"Look at this picture, what do you think?"

"We're completely alone, you know that?" I stretch out my legs and push back against the big chair, a chair comfortable and elegant enough to cradle collectors about to part with their millions. Sebastian pulls a small canvas from the bins and props it against the wall. It's a Paddy Nolan painting, a pale wavy wash of green on blue.

"Early Nolan," I say, letting the sensual colors soothe me. Sebastian brought me here after one of our first lunches. "Remember when you brought me here that time after lunch when we were pretending to be just friends? Did you want to fuck me then?" The champagne, the silence around us, the locked doors all focus my intensity.

"His prices have slipped a little, but this is a good one," Sebastian says, stepping sideways to avoid my hand reaching out toward him.

"I was so turned on! Remember? You were so seductive, standing back here." I stretch out and stroke his elusive leg under the expensive worsted of his blue suit.

"Oliver Remsen wants to sell it, he's planning to buy one of the new David Salle pictures at Mary Boone's. Everything has to be new, all these collectors want is to have the latest thing."

"He can't have both?" I've managed to draw Sebastian closer and I slide my hand under his jacket, hiking up my skirt and sliding down in the chair. "What if we'd made love right then?"

"He's one of those collectors who doesn't like to buy without selling." Now Sebastian has moved next to me and lets my hands press and gently squeeze. "I don't know which is worse, the ones like that or the others who can't stop buying and end up building these repulsive private museums to house their so-called collections. Mmmmm, what are you doing?"

"Are you going to buy it?" I turn in the chair so that he's standing between my legs.

"No, I sell it for him to another collector. It's not easy with a painting like this, because it's no longer fashionable."

"What do you take?" I sit up to undo his belt buckle.

"The dealer's official commission is twenty percent; it varies. Look at this." Sebastian turns away from me, slips the Nolan back in the bin, and leans a larger George Mallet canvas against the wall.

"Did you ever sell that Ernst? Remember, the one I liked that first day? The day I wanted to make love to you right here?" Sebastian has moved back close enough to my chair so that I can stroke him again. I lift my legs, running them up his so that my skirt falls back to my waist, and resume my ministrations. "There's no one else here, Sebastian, we're alone."

"A wonderful painting." Sebastian's attention is still on the

Mallet, whose delicate wash of powerful color makes the Nolan look like art students' work.

"How many of those do you have?" I've now succeeded in undoing his pants.

"Four or five." Sebastian steps out of his pants as I pull him toward me, but he's preoccupied. "Of course, I got the pick." "Do you really think the Nolan's that weak?" I pull Sebastian down so that he's kneeling between my legs on the chair, but he stands up again to take off his jacket and shoes.

"I certainly wouldn't pull out the Mallet when you're trying to sell it," I say, unbuttoning my blouse. "I've been wanting to do this ever since that first lunch."

"Don't worry," Sebastian says, pushing me back against the chair. "If there's one thing I know how to do, it's sell a painting." The chair tips dangerously backward and as it tilts I slide down onto the floor with Sebastian between my legs. As he enters me I can feel my ankle brushing against the edge of the Mallet canvas.

"There are a lot of things you know how to do," I whisper. "Like fucking me." I push my legs against him to avoid the canvas and pray it doesn't fall over on us. My skirt presses into my back and my head bumps against the floor as Sebastian pounds into me, finally echoing my desire. Out of the corner of my eye I can see the Mallet threateningly balanced above us.

4 "You'll never guess who I slept with last night," Julie says in a lowered voice, the sexy murmur she uses for secrets. She sips at a glass of red wine and picks at her salad. "The head of the English Lit department at Yale, do you know him? He lives in New Haven." She giggles as if sleeping with the head of the English department at Yale was just about the funniest thing anyone could do.

"Married?" I ask. My salad is finished; I spread butter on a piece of crusty Italian bread.

"Isn't everyone?"

"Julie, you are so bad!" I say. "What's the poor man's name?"

Julie laughs and tosses her hair. "Harvey West," she says. "And you're right, he thinks he's in love with me."

"How could he not be?" I laugh like an admiring conspirator. Silently I say a small prayer for the emotional balance and mental health of Harvey West, wherever he is, with his drab but faithful wife and his innocent children.

"I only did it for Samantha," she says. Julie is halfway through a second glass of wine, and as if she guessed my thoughts, she pushes out her lip in an enchanting pout in case I'm angry with her. "She's decided she wants to go to Yale, isn't that exciting? And Harvey promised to help!" She sees that I'm not angry and throws back her head, laughing her musical child's laugh, rapturous at the thought of the super-human efforts Harvey West will make to get Samantha into Yale. A man at the table near the window stares across at us while his date talks on obliviously. Julie, sensing the male interest, turns a brief and radiant smile in his direction.

"Please don't tell Samantha, though," she says now, leaning

forward and shutting out the rest of the world. "I don't want her to know that I slept her way to the top." I giggle, and the man at the other table turns back to his conversation.

"A girl has to get into college somehow," Julie says. As she shrugs her shoulders, a phrase of Sebastian's pops into my mind. It had been his reaction when I told him some of the things that not everyone knows about my father.

"You can also sleep your way to the bottom," he said.

Sebastian doesn't really approve of Julie, and if he heard us talk about him he'd be horrified. There's nothing I don't tell her, and sometimes it's in sharing it with Julie that my own experience comes to seem interesting or funny instead of just plain painful. She's all dazzle and sophistication. She can pick any lock, and bake a Lady Baltimore cake from scratch. She can wiggle her ears, she can drink two bottles of wine and not show it, and she can raise a teenage daughter and look ravishing all the time, as if it was easy, as if it was all easy. Even her disasters are exciting. When she was married she had a skiing accident at St. Moritz that left her with a permanent bad back. Doctors prescribe fancy painkillers, and she still gets letters from Prince David of somewhere or other, who fell in love with her while she was in the hospital.

After lunch, we walk down to Bloomingdale's. Julie is wearing a bright green dress that throws her dark hair and pale skin into vivid relief—and that makes every woman we pass resolve to buy a bright green dress. When Julie shops, there is no soul-destroying leafing through the racks of dress after dress as the spirit sags and hangers squeak. Salesladies leap to do her bidding. Whatever she picks from the rack is somehow just right, the clothes look sensational on her slim body with her dark and light coloring. All I ever look for are clothes that will make me feel like someone else.

In the dressing room, I quickly slough off my blue linen blazer and gray skirt, peeling down to the matching cotton underwear I wore because I knew we were going shopping. The mirror throws back an image of my firm, curvy body and long, coppery brown hair. Too fat, I think, too messy. Summer has bleached strawberry-blond streaks into my bangs and I shake them forward and stand up straighter to flatten my stomach. My clothes are in a heap on the floor. If I never see them again, that's all right with me.

Julie reaches down to the hem of her bright green dress, and in one sinuous motion pulls it over her head. She shakes out her black hair as the dress crumples to the floor. Underneath it she is naked. Her body is slender, with small breasts and a line of pale skin across her buttocks from the protection of a tiny bikini bottom.

"That line's still there," she says, rubbing at the transition from pale to paler flesh with one pink fingernail. She seems perfectly unaware of the electrifying presence of her body. As she slips on one dress after another from a stack of hangers proffered by an obsequious saleslady, she eyes herself critically in the mirror and rejects each one. They all look great. I struggle into the kind of flowery shirtwaist I favor because I think it is "feminine" and "pretty."

"That's *suburban*, Elizabeth," Julie says. "It's time for you to stop dressing like a little girl." She ties my sash in the back. "You have a terrific body, try to look as if you own it, don't slump!"

"You sound like my mother."

"Well, it's true. Either you're wearing clothes that look like uniforms from the schools you hated"—she waves at my clothes in the corner—"or you're wearing these *jeune fille* numbers. I want more for you. You should turn heads! You should rock the room when you walk in!" Julie is wearing a black dress with a gathered hip yoke that looks as if it was cut for her.

"That's how *you* look," I say, untying the flowered dress, which I've come to hate. She's right, it's boring.

"Wait a second, try on this one!" She slides the black dress off her shoulders, steps out of it, and hands it to me.

"But it looks so wonderful on you!"

"Black isn't really my color, but with your hair . . ." Julie strokes my hair; electricity fans it out toward her hand in a triangle of webby silk.

"It'll be too tight around the hips."

"Shut up and try it." Julie has already turned away and is pulling a slinky tube of lipstick-red jersey over her head. I unzip the flowered dress, take it off, and, trying not to slump, step into the black one. As the silk lining slides along my skin, I can feel it fitting. The angled yoke rests gently against my hips and the light wool challis falls into place from my shoulders.

"See, that's great on you!" Julie has turned back to me. "You look fabulous; that's a terrific haircut, did John give you that haircut?" John is Julie's hairdresser; he adores her and he tolerates me because I am her friend.

I nod, because miraculously Julie's right. The black dress creates an aura of self-possession and elegance. In the mirror I look like someone else, a restrained sort of young woman, the kind of woman who would never get involved with a married man or binge on glazed doughnuts from the supermarket, or need an abortion, or not know what she wants to do with her life, or live like a perennial student with her parents' cast-off furniture.

"Oooh," I say, trying not to give in to vanity. "I look so upper-class, like some friend of Melissa Smith's."

"You've got her on the brain. I don't know why I'm helping you dress, Sebastian's so besotted he probably doesn't care how you look." She stops speaking for a moment. "Casey never cared how you looked, did he?" she asks.

"Fuck him," I say. I don't want to think about Patrick Casey, about the past. "Why bring him up?"

"It's a nice dress." Julie shrugs her shoulders and changes the subject.

"It is nice." I turn, trying to quiet painful memories. "Then why doesn't he leave her?"

"He probably would if you told him to. Men need to be told what to do. You just can't let them know that you know that they need to be told what to do. Here, try this." Julie unloops a chain of uneven gold links from her throat and puts it over my head. Casey didn't need to be told what to do, I think.

"Good," she says. "We'll have to get you a gold chain."

5 It's a bitter December night, the fir trees along Park Avenue are lit with starry bulbs, the moth-eaten Salvation Army Santa Clauses have appeared on the corners in midtown, where ladies who have just charged $5,000 dresses refuse quarters to the beggars outside Bergdorf's and Bonwit's. The opening night of Daddy's first retrospective at the Whitney Museum is a major event of the art-world season. Tonight the ladies are wearing their dresses: columns of velvet, clouds of organza. They skid on the ice outside the museum in their gold-and-silver evening slippers. Searchlights sweep the night sky, and banners with our name on them flap in the cold wind.

Our parents eat with the museum trustees and a few collectors. Andrew and I have a hamburger at Melon's. Those museum dinners are too painful for Andrew; he can't keep his mouth shut while the collectors drool about their possessions: horses, houses, young wives, and Fairfax Cole paintings. Andrew is still too much on edge to be polite sometimes, even though he takes a flesh-colored lithium capsule every morning and has ever since his bad time in college. Being fresh to collectors is not allowed. Unlike writers and musicians, visual artists are entirely dependent for their livelihood on a small group of rich patrons who buy most of their work. Sometimes it's a dozen, usually it's four or five.

"I hope the collectors are enjoying their million-dollar veal," I say as Andrew pours ketchup on our order of fries and swigs a beer.

"They always get their money's worth from Dad," he says. "He knows how to act like an artist."

"Flamboyant but deferential."

26 | "He's forgotten all about the Modern, remember that? He's acting as if he wanted this retrospective at the Whitney all along, that's what gets me about it. What happened to his feelings? Why can't he express his disappointment? He's taking hind tit."

"How *can* he act? He's not allowed to sulk." Daddy had lobbied for years to have his show at the Museum of Modern Art. "He has to pretend that what he has is what he wants." He had failed. In our family, disappointment and triumph often go together.

"Right, everything's for the best in this best of all possible worlds! He's Candide!" Andrew sounded furious. We were all afraid of Andrew's anger, which could explode in a volatile flash or drive him into paralyzed silence. Maybe this was why he had gotten away with treating Karen so badly, or rather, maybe this was why she was always there, waiting for him to come back, ready to take him back and live with him again and get engaged to him again. Ready to get dumped.

"It's more like P. T. Barnum," I say gently, trying to disagree without riling him. "Forget failure, the show must go on!"

"Until the next failure," Andrew says.

But as Andrew and I follow our parents into the museum later, I feel a crazy surge of pride in our brash family and the way we look. We do put on a good show. My handsome parents, arm in arm, are flanked by their handsome children. Who knows that every year at tax time my father puts the house on the market, or that he drinks so much that he can't get up the stairs sometimes, or that my mother sleeps with the gardener when he's away . . . and whose business is it? She wears her long hair in a glossy bun, and her black dress is sedately beaded across the shoulders. My father wears a dinner jacket and red satin suspenders. A chamber-music quartet, two women with long black hair and long black dresses and two men with beards, plays Vivaldi in a corner of the museum's granite lobby as we float in through the doors from the icy night. The crowd hushes. Then there is a scattering of applause and more applause as my father makes his majestic way across the floor and toward the elevators to the exhibition rooms, where he has spent the last weeks bullying the curators and staff. At this moment, I almost wish Sebastian were here to see us. I teased him about the opening, and said that I didn't think I could behave if he brought Melissa. He promised he wouldn't be there. My relief at knowing I won't have to face Mr. and Mrs. Sebastian Smith is pierced with a fragment of regret.

Upstairs, I see that my father's attention to the installation has paid off. His paintings, the portraits and party scenes, the landscapes and sea vistas, gleam against pale gray walls. My father's work is representational, even sentimental, but because the canvases are big and because of his impressionistic blocks of color, they are quite different from the more literal nostalgia of Andrew Wyeth or Norman Rockwell. He knew and studied with the early abstract expressionists, and his work has some of their raw force—he's able to give the passion of the abstract back to the specific. That's the combination that makes his work so popular, I think. It's easy to like. It's not intimidating or confusing, but at the same time it has a cultural whammy— an unmistakable high seriousness. His collectors are able to enjoy the work, hang it without fear, and at the same time feel that they are important appreciators of that mystical entity called Art. Grouped together, the energy of the paintings seems to be released. Alone they are charming vignettes, celebrations of a moment. Together they merge into an authoritative view of the world which transcends each pretty scene.

The lobby crowd has filtered up the stairs, swarming around Daddy as he stops to greet the chief curator. The paintings are only visible through a moving kaleidoscope of shifting bodies and talking heads. Whitney shows bring out the outlandish and the grotesque. There's a woman wrapped in white feathers with a matching headdress, and another whose headdress of peacock feathers vibrates like antennae as she mingles with the crowd. There are the pretty young women and their much older, much richer husbands. I catch sight of Bettina Van Doren Antmeter Sandoz and her latest marital acquisition,

Colombian trillionaire Carlos Sandoz. He's stooped and leathery, with carefully combed white hair around a tanned bald spot. She looks like a South American bird in plum and pink satin crisscrossed around her body and a collar of rubies and diamonds. Julie says Bettina started in Paris as one of Madame Claude's stable of "girls" and that her secret is tremendous vaginal agility, which men—especially older men—can't resist. Bettina's talking to another decked-out beauty, Binney Black. When Binney's husband, eighty-year-old real-estate tycoon Jack Black, died last year, she inherited his fortune and married her personal trainer, a young stud who is standing next to her, looking restless in a tight evening jacket.

Andrew and I weave toward the east rooms greeting people, smiling and eavesdropping on fragments of conversation. I stop as Andrew kisses Lydia Hutchinson, a willowy Sotheby's French furniture expert whom he once dated. "Such a *remarkable*," I hear behind me. "She's never had an eye, you know. She's an A list collector with a B list collection." I turn to see Gray Anderson, a small, dapper dealer talking with a woman I don't know, but before I can move toward them, Andrew is pulling me forward again.

"The Kelly was too difficult for them," I hear another voice to my right. "The decorator said nothing *green!*" I don't recognize the speaker, a thin woman in a black dress swathed in a huge embroidered shawl. Andrew and I slowly slalom our way through the crowd, stopping to talk with my Greenwich Village neighbors the Bayers.

"Lizzie dear, you look positively enervating!" Caroline gushes in her upper-class drawl. She always gets long words slightly wrong. Over her shoulder I see the tall, Ichabod Crane-like figure and buck teeth of Philip Goff, my boss's boss, stooping down to ogle the low neckline of a young woman who seems about to leap up on him. I hope he's registering my connection to this glamorous night.

"You too," I say, leaning over to let her kiss the air on each side of my face. As Ernst prospers, Caroline glows, with golden skin perpetually caressed by Caribbean or Alpine sun, golden jewelry, and burnished hair. I remember her dark, gawky good looks from school days; now she looks just like Melissa Smith. Against an opposite wall I see thick blond hair and the back of a red dress.

"Uh oh," Andrew says to me.

"I'll take care of it, I *like* Karen."

She looks so sad when she turns to kiss me that I'm afraid Karen has heard us. She was stupid to come, but then I see the photographer hovering behind her and remember that she had to come. Karen writes about art for a living. "It's a terrific installation," she says.

"Daddy had to do all the work himself."

"It was worth it." We turn to look at the nearest picture, a small oil of my father's favorite Labrador, Marcus Garvey, on the lawn of a house we rented in Maine one summer. Marcus is the son of Sable of Teatown out of Arden's Bridget, and my father never lets us forget it.

"You know I came tonight thinking that this show should have been at the Modern," Karen says, "but now I'm not so sure."

"It *was* too bad!" I remember Andrew's scorn for Daddy's meliorism.

"But it looks good here, after all. The Whitney was started as a family museum, and your father paints in that tradition."

"What's the deal with the Modern, anyway?"

"I think it's the essays your father wrote attacking Alfred Barr and the Modern trustees for being slow to buy the abstract expressionists. They *were* slow, but no one thanks the messenger."

"But that was years ago, when I was a kid!"

"True, but Bill Rubin was Barr's protégé. His influence is still felt."

"Barr's dead."

"It doesn't really matter; defending his ideas is a matter of honor at the Modern." Animated by her own opinions, Karen looks like a different person, her face is flushed and dimples punctuate her smile.

"Family feuds," I say. "They should all be working to-gether."

"The art world is so small, there's a lot at stake," Karen says. She turns to her photographer, and I wander back downstairs for a second glass of wine, passing my friend Ingrid, who's wearing a red embroidered Chinese robe which makes her look like a ship's figurehead. She's talking in a low, private voice to a big tweedy man, and beyond him I see Oliver Remsen looking bored. Remsen is one of Daddy's big-fish collectors, a man who has given five Cole paintings to the Whitney.

"Two gin-and-tonics, no lime . . ." I'm chilled, frozen in my tracks by the familiar voice at the other end of the bar. I turn and my heart flips over, because there's Sebastian in his impeccable evening clothes, leaning forward to collect two drinks, one for Mr. Sebastian Smith and one for Mrs. Sebastian Smith.

"Sebastian?" For a blink, as he turns and sees me standing there in the black dress I see all the conflict of his disintegrating marriage in his long, elegant face.

"Elizabeth, oh, I'm sorry." He stammers. I stare, speechless. Did he think he wouldn't see me? Did he think he could just come and avoid me all night? Men are so *dumb*!

"She insisted, and I thought there would be so many people . . ." He looks like Melissa's cowed errand boy dispatched to get her a drink while she chats about art with her important Junior League pals.

"You didn't think at all, or you wouldn't be here." Sebastian takes a step backward as I advance on him.

"I couldn't stay away," he says, straightening up and smiling a little. Watching him recover his poise is like watching a yacht right itself in heavy seas. "And I was right, you look so beautiful! I had to see you." I can't help smiling back a little, because I feel beautiful and I'm half glad that he's here. We edge away from the bar toward a wall, separated by the two tall drinks which he holds in front of him like Tristan's sword.

Behind him a painting of the brown shingle house in New Hampshire where we spent some summers shimmers on the wall like a window to the past.

"Did you *have* to?" I still feel nervous and betrayed. To my family's night of triumph, my man has been brought against his will, led docilely by his official wife. I have caught him acting the dutiful husband. "Would you run and get me a drink, dear?" "Oh, of course, dear." He probably didn't even have to ask what she wanted.

"I'm sorry, baby." Sebastian looks worried again, he's caught in the female cross fire.

"I don't mind *you* being here, but did you have to bring the Lady Melissa? Jesus!"

At this explosion of indignation, Sebastian starts to laugh and color comes back to his cheeks. It's not a tragedy, after all, it's a farce! He bends over slightly to conceal his mirth and the ice sloshes around in the drinks, spilling one over the lip of the glass and onto the polished floor.

"Clumsy ox!" I'm laughing now, too. "You'd better give *her* that one."

"I just *love* you," Sebastian says. "Your indignation is wonderful. The Lady Melissa!"

"The drinks, Sebastian!" They've both begun to overflow as he moves toward me. "Sebastian, she's going to be very unhappy with you." I sense that other people are beginning to look, and then peripherally I see Melissa's fine, porcelain face turning toward us from the other side of the room. Where is her gin-and-tonic? Her errand boy is late! Abandoning all propriety, and winning my heart forever, Sebastian puts both arms around me, still holding a drink in each hand, and gives me a long, cool kiss on the lips. The cold glasses press against my back as I stand in his embrace.

"I've got to go, or she won't let me out again," he says as he draws away. "When can I see you?"

"You're seeing me."

"Don't tease."

"Are you sure you'll have any free time?"

"Tomorrow?" he says, not moving. I can feel Melissa steaming toward us through the crowd, and I nod assent.

"I love you." Sebastian mouths the words as he backs off and disappears into the press of people, stopping to smile at Gray Anderson. Melissa's distraught face has been blocked from my view by a crowd standing in front of a Greenwich Village street scene, the largest painting in the show.

I pick up a fresh glass of wine and start for a corner where Oliver Remsen is talking to Julie. Norma Skales wafts past me, a wraith in a black Ungaro. Her pale face and Charles Addams center-parted hair have a pasty, surreal look which was once ephemeral beauty, a beauty so compelling that the great abstract expressionists, de Kooning and Pollock, were in love with her. Daddy was, too, before he married my mother. But Norma married a rich man from Chicago and began to collect the work of her old lovers. Now the husband is dead, his children by an earlier marriage have tied up the estate in endless court battles, and Norma drifts from party to party like the ghost of happier times.

"Good work!" Julie whispers to me as I approach. "I think everyone in the room saw *that* performance."

"Do you think *she* noticed?" I want to hear it. Oliver Remsen with his leathery skin and red bow tie can wait.

"I think that boy is in deep, deep trouble," Julie says.

Across the room I catch a flash of Melissa and Sebastian. She has the glossy satin back of her evening dress to me and her conversation is punctuated by angry gestures which rattle the sparkling bracelets on her thin arms. He's backed up against the wall, and I can't see his face. I push through the crowd and go back upstairs to where my parents are still surrounded by congratulators and admirers: curators, collectors, dealers, and critics. There are few artists at other artists' openings. Daddy nods and beams as people salute him; he has never been uncomfortable with success. Whatever she feels in private, my mother always seems to merge with my father at public events. They become one two-headed personality, Mr. and Mrs. Fairfax Cole, the-artist-and-his-wife.

"You look great, Mummy," I say, squeezing her arm through black velvet, but she's distracted by the conversation my father is having with Democratic Senator Jack Bullmore about pending legislation to give artists a royalty each time their paintings are resold. Theodore North, a major Miami collector, is also waiting to speak with Daddy. My mother stands there like a horse in the gate, ready to inject the enhancing phrase or smile her famous-beauty smile. Other women never get near my father in public.

I wander through the emptying rooms looking for Andrew. In the smaller north room, dominated by one of the protruding trapezoidal windows Marcel Breuer used to give this building the look of a granite centaur, I step back behind a wall to avoid Tamara Brush, a tiny woman whose dancer's body is swathed in purple jersey, which parts to expose her back down to the buttocks. Tamara turns away from me, too. There were five years when she was my father's favorite model. Five years of veiled anger and tears at the dinner table and the echoes of my parents' voices fighting upstairs. Five years of my mother threatening divorce and my father trying to pass it all off as casual. We all breathed a sigh of relief when she married a man who seems to own most of Texas. There are strands of gray in Tamara's black slicked-back hair. On the other side of the room I see that Melissa still has Sebastian pinned to the wall.

Andrew is near the elevators chatting with Amanda Plum, a bouncy woman who works with him at Dunhill, Taylor, and who I'm sure has a crush on him. Behind them is a watercolor my father did recently of Marcus Garvey's littermate Booker. Booker was killed by a truck out on the Connecticut Turnpike three years ago on one of his forays after sex or food, but his soft, sympathetic doggy eyes and velvety jowls live on in pigment. Booker was my dog for a while. He slept on my bed at night and waited for me to come home from school. Now he's

dead. The crowd is thinning, the important collectors have
gone home. The pictures come back to life on the walls as
the people filter out.

"Your father looks as if he's in heaven," Amanda says. She's
wearing a low-cut blue dress and standing as close to Andrew
as she dares.

"Pig heaven." Andrew's had too much to drink. As he takes
in Amanda's dress, I put a hand on his arm. Don't do it,
Andrew, I think. Not worth it, Andrew.

"He deserves it, it took a while." I'm always softening Andrew's grudge against our parents. I don't want people to know
what it's really like under that veneer of family harmony. He
doesn't seem to give a fuck. Across the room I see Melissa
hustling Sebastian toward the door. He looks tired and suddenly I feel profoundly tired. It's past midnight, the bartenders
downstairs are putting away the bottles in liquor boxes and
folding the tables. Tomorrow morning I have to be at work,
acting perky and pretending that I don't spend most of my
time daydreaming about Sebastian or wondering what to have
for lunch or how early I can leave. The lights in the back
rooms are being turned off.

"Come on, kid brother," I say. "Let's blow this joint." Andrew kisses Amanda, gently disentangles himself from her fare-
well embrace, and heads with me for the stairs. He stumbles
at the top step and I take his arm, remembering our triumphal
family entry, the applause, the pride. Out on the street an icy
wind blasts up Madison Avenue, cutting through my dress and
coat. As we stand there shivering and waiting for a cab, I envy
Sebastian and Melissa their warm apartment a few blocks away.
I try not to hope that he's miserable.

6 I pencil in a 24-point head in Cheltenham Bold, my favorite typeface: SWINGING SHINGLES. We're doing a story on new houses with old styles in the Hamptons, the kind of story we do more of since the reign of Goff. I break the page and rule boxes for photographs of the house and the architect, a trendy fellow with offices in Northern California.

"That's the shits!" Judith Grimes-Gurewitz says from over my shoulder where she's been standing in uncharacteristic silence. "It sounds like a fucking disease! Richard," she shrieks across the room to the editor's cubicle, "change the architecture head!" Richard doesn't respond, but he's heard her—with *her* voice everyone in the greater downtown area has heard her. She gives my shoulder a squeeze, her long red fingernails dig into my skin. "That layout's okay," she says as she moves back to her desk. I stretch and wait for the new character count, too tired to wonder why she's being nice to me this morning.

After I got home from the Whitney and hung up the black dress, put on an old flannel nightgown and crawled into bed, I lay awake thinking about the fight I hoped Melissa and Sebastian were having. I've never been in their apartment, but I've imagined it so often that it's as familiar to me as my own. Of course I couldn't sleep. This morning my mouth tasted like cotton and my head throbbed. It took three aspirins and four cups of coffee to get out of the house.

"Work all day, work all night . . ." Richard is humming as he dumps the new head on my desk. ARCHITECTURE: GOLDEN OLDIES.

"Pretty good," I say, and he grins.

"Let's have it," the Grimy Guru sirens from her desk. "No fraternizing!" Her thin lips curl slightly to show that this is a joke, but it doesn't sound like a joke. I wonder if she has a crush on Richard. *Antics* is losing money and I suspect that the pet-food tycoon is about to replace the redoubtable Grimy with an uptown editor, someone he'll raid with great fanfare from Hearst or Condé Nast.

"Grimy never lets us out of her sight," Richard sings to the same tune as he turns away from my desk. My phone rings.

"Elizabeth." Sebastian's voice sounds as if the night's arguments had worn it out.

"Hi," I say, trying to count characters and at least look as if I'm drawing. Grimy is glaring at me from the front of the room.

"You're not angry?"

"Unh-unh," I mutter. Richard's looking over at me, too. The longer head means moving down one of the boxes. I erase and redraw it.

"Can you meet me at the Oyster Bar at twelve?" I know this means that Sebastian is calling me from uptown, probably from his apartment, which explains the whispery voice. To get to the Oyster Bar in time I'll have to leave before eleven-thirty, and it's almost eleven now. Of course, I'll do it.

"Should I be angry?" I stall. Richard and Judith *will* both be angry. We're closing the issue today.

"Christ, what a night."

"Really bad?" I draw the new rules, trying to make it look as if I'm talking to an important supplier or another editor. Grimy starts over toward my desk, but providentially her phone rings and she turns back to answer it.

"As bad as it gets; at least I hope that's as bad as it gets."

"What did she say?" Grimy is hanging up now and starting for my desk.

"I can't talk," Sebastian says. *He* can't talk!

"Okay, see you there," I say, quickly hanging up just as Ms. Grimes-Gurewitz arrives.

"When you're finished with that, look at these," she says, throwing a sheaf of photographs on my desk. "The San Francisco pictures we took for the cover are excrement! Shit! Can you draw something?"

"We're doing a cover on this joker?"

"Elizabeth, he's the most exciting young architect in the country today, and besides"—she delivers this absolutely deadpan—"he's designing a house in the Napa Valley for Philip Goff."

"Rrrrright," I say. Grimy and I actually exchange a smile. There's nothing like a common adversary.

As I flip through the uninspired photographs of San Francisco, I alternate between hope and despair. A sketch *would* be better, but I've never done a cover before. What if Sebastian announces that we can't see each other anymore? I know how to draw San Francisco, and shingle style did start there in a way with Maybeck and Julia Morgan. Did Melissa give him some kind of ultimatum? With Sebastian I'm always either reliving the past or anticipating the future. When you're in love with someone who is married, there's no daily life, no practical application of feelings. There are the moments of stolen passion, there are the possibilities, and that's it.

"Let's get a drink," Sebastian says. I lean forward to hear him. The roar of other voices in the room is like a tangible liquid substance overflowing the tables and lapping against the tiled columns.

"White wine and a seafood salad," I shout at him.

"Don't you even want to look at the menu?" Sebastian's face is pale, his voice so low I have to lean into the table. "There are usually specials, they go down to the Fulton Fish Market every morning."

"I want to hear what happened last night!"

"Can't you wait a minute? Let me have a drink, for God's sake."

"I've been going nuts. You're not the only one affected by this. Please."

"You're right." Sebastian is interrupted by the waiter, and

he orders for both of us. Then he puts his head down as if to gather memories. "Where do I start . . . she was furious and hurt and . . ."

"About one lousy kiss?"

"If you want to hear what happened . . ."

"Sorry. I'm listening."

"She said she didn't care what I did in private, that she knew I had been unfaithful to her, that I had probably always been unfaithful to her, but she couldn't stand seeing it in public, in front of people she knows. She felt humiliated."

"Did my name come up in the conversation?" I'm too intent on what Sebastian is saying to ask if he has always been unfaithful to his wife, and if so with whom?

"She's not blind. I'm not sure what she's going to do."

"Too bad," I say. Fuck her, I think.

"It *is* too bad. She said it was degrading and cruel, she accused me of not caring about the children and lying and all kinds of things, and then at the end she collapsed and cried and said she loved me more than ever and she'd do anything to keep the marriage together."

"Did you sleep with her?"

"It was a terrible night."

"It must be hard," I say, "being loved so much."

"Melissa and I have been together a long time, it's very painful. Can you understand that?"

"I understand the pain, I don't understand the confusion."

"She's the mother of my children."

"That sounds like something out of a Victorian novel."

"I don't mean it to sound that way, but my little girls . . ." His voice breaks and he stares down at the dressing on his plate. "How can I leave my children?"

"You wouldn't be leaving them. Why does this all have to be so melodramatic?" Across the table I see that his face is crumpling; to control his mouth he takes a swig of Scotch. "Oh, baby," I say. "It's okay, I'll love you whatever you do."

"I'm glad you said that." He manages a melancholy laugh.

I pretend not to see that there are tears in his eyes. We both pick at our salads in silence.

"Do you really think this is right?" I ask after a while. "You're leading this kind of empty life with a woman you don't love. Is that so good for the children?"

Sebastian shrugs. He seems to be shrinking, slumping down and getting smaller and smaller, as if he wishes he could just disappear and leave all these problems behind in some noisy midtown restaurant.

"I don't know," he says in a voice I can hardly hear. "Love doesn't last and marriages do. I'm not the first man who has ever gone through this! The worst thing is that I know what the children would choose if they could. Children want their parents to stay together no matter what. That's what Melissa wants, too."

"But children adjust and survive. Look at you! Look around you. Plenty of couples are divorced and their children are fine. I think I would have been better off if my parents *had* divorced. Why does it have to be such a big deal when it's you and Melissa?"

"Maybe it's because I thought we'd be different. It's hard to admit that we're just like everyone else . . ." He trails off.

"It's hard for everyone. What you have to remember is that you're in control. You're the one who is going to make the decision. If you waver, it will just be harder for all of us."

"I can't make a decision right now. Please don't make me feel worse, I've already heard enough about what a shit I am today. I promised Melissa that nothing will happen right away."

"Am I supposed to wait until she's ready to let you go?"

"You're not supposed to do anything you don't want to do." Now Sebastian looks as if he's going to cry again. Of course, the terrible fact is that I'm willing to wait forever—or until Melissa lets go, whichever comes first. To me Sebastian is the only man in the world, and Melissa wanting him back so badly makes him more desirable. I know what she means when she breaks down and says that she loves him more than ever—just when she ought to be hating him! The prospect of losing him adds to his value. Now I reach over and stroke his handsome, troubled face. "Let's go back to my apartment," I say. "Maybe I can cheer you up somehow."

Making love to Sebastian is always intense, very intense, but this afternoon I cling to him as if he were a fraying lifeline that might keep me afloat in some turbulent, swirling oceanic current. For a minute we are together at the absolute center of the universe and all the other people in my block and on Bleecker and Houston and in the Village and the whole city and all the galaxy of distant planets revolve around our spinning senses.

Afterward Sebastian lays a cool palm against my forehead. I can feel the smoothness of his signet ring against my skin and smell his faint, salty sweat. In the stripes of sunlight from the window, motes of dust glisten and tumble like early dry snowflakes.

"You're right," he says after a while. "This can't go on." He's right, but it does.

"You're sure this is what you want to do?" Casey had asked.

We stood together at China Beach, looking out across the Bay toward the Golden Gate and the Marin headlands.

"I don't see any alternative." I had flown out to see him, to tell him. A flock of sailboats like colored birds spread out in a V toward the bridge and then one by one turned back toward Sausalito.

"I've told you what they are."

"It's just not practical! I live in New York and I have a good job and family and friends there. You live out here, you've always lived out here. If one of us moved because of this, we'd feel too awful about it. I don't see how it could work out." The truth is, I was scared.

"You don't want to risk it?" he said. Wind off the Bay

whipped around our heads and I shivered. It was supposed to be summer. How could I live in a place where you shivered in the summer?

"It's just because you're so Catholic, Patrick Casey," I said. "People do this all the time."

"Other people," he said. A pale green oil tanker plowed through the potato patch of chop and currents, leaving a fishing boat yawing in its huge wake.

"You're taking it so hard! Everyone I know has done this, it's even legal." I was trying to make him laugh and hold me again, but instead, he turned away and looked out at the water.

7 I pick my way through the icy slush along Houston toward Mercer, where Ingrid's loft sprawls across the top floor of an old dry-goods warehouse. After a snowstorm the habitual city noise level—a New Age symphony of sirens, horns, and voices—is subdued. Instead, there are the calming, practical chunks and scrapes of people digging out. I've accepted Ingrid's invitation to drop by and see a new painting, but I'm dreading her monologue on her own brilliant techniques and fabulous creativity, a diatribe usually accompanied by a huge mug of bitter herbal tea.

"I gave up wine and coffee a year ago," she'll say. "This Pau d'Arco tea rights the yeast imbalance from all those antibiotics we take; it's a blend I get from my psychic healer," or some such claptrap, as if her discovery of metabolic purity obligates us all to get healthy. I know her psychic healer charges $350 a visit. I would rather be with Sebastian. I would rather be drinking red wine and schmoozing at Julie's. I would even rather be working on my San Francisco cover sketches. Drawing the city makes me wonder about Casey. I don't even know if he still lives there.

I ring a bell in the corrugated-iron wall of the ornate façade, which is covered with graffiti and decades of New York soot, and wait to be buzzed up the three flights of grimy stairs to the perfect north light and pared-down rooms where Ingrid lives and works. I stomp up the dark staircase boiling with resentment. Ingrid herself, in a flowing purple caftan, beckons me through the door.

"How do you like it?" she asks, waving a big arm toward the center of the wall opposite the door, where a giant canvas hangs under dramatic multiple spotlights. Ingrid isn't much for preliminaries. The painting is a snarl of red and black acrylic; the mess that Ingrid keeps out of her life and her loft explodes into her work.

"It's good, Ingrid," I say, "very strong." Turning toward her under the lights, I notice that there's someone else in the room, a man sitting quietly and watching our little drama from the wings, lounging in the comfort of one of Ingrid's leather armchairs.

"This is Elizabeth Cole, Ed Lissner," Ingrid says, with the air of making an important presentation. Ed Lissner is older than we are, with brown thinning hair and a big, blocky body, and as I smile I recognize him as the man who was talking with Ingrid at Daddy's Whitney opening, and I wonder if he is a new boyfriend of Ingrid's—the man who will change her mind about men. Ed Lissner doesn't look like the kind of schmuck who breaks hearts.

"I love the texture," I say, staring with self-conscious intensity at the painting. I move closer to the canvas, as if to examine in detail every amazing brushstroke. Two more positive comments and I will have satisfied Ingrid's vanity; then I can thump down in one of the comfortable chairs and ease my aching back. A bowl of fruit and a couple of cheeses in waxy white paper are laid out on the slate coffee table next to a bottle of white wine. Ed Lissner is a good gastronomic influence at least. I move in farther, seeing that Ingrid has scraped away at the canvas with her palette knife, creating a mottled effect which makes the surface seem to fall away from the paint and projects the fiery reds toward the spectator.

"There's a lot of depth," I say, "you're getting away from the flat plane. When did you finish it?"

"Yesterday." But she still stands next to me expectantly.

"It's a shift of direction for you." Ed Lissner's voice is deep, with a slight Midwestern softness. "The flame projects well, you've really made it burn. There's a solid physical reference."

Looking at the painting, I see that Ed Lissner has a point. The reds at the center of the canvas generate a heat which is magnified by what Ingrid has done with the background. Smart guy, I think, he's gotten me off the hook. Ingrid, sated, perches on a chair next to him and I sink into soft comfort.

"Do you live in the city?" I ask Ed. Instead of answering, he leans over and passes the plate of cheese, which he has cut into neat wedges, stripped of its white rind, and spread on the crackers. Past his shoulders, through Ingrid's high windows, I can see the view to the south, the ornate towers of Wall Street and the mammoth double domino of the World Trade Center.

"Ed teaches at NYU," Ingrid says. "I met him when I had that show at the Loeb Center." She flicks her long hair over her shoulder and reaches for the cheese. Everything about Ingrid is as big as her ego. She accentuates her Wagnerian looks by wearing flowing clothes, leaving her hair long and loose, and punctuating her conversation with operatic gestures. "That was the show the Met bought from the first time they acquired one of my large works," she says. "Ed lives on Eighth Street, near you."

"What do you teach?" I speak directly to Ed, hoping to interrupt Ingrid's habit of answering all questions whether or not they are directed to her.

"Art," Ingrid answers. "He teaches one of the few scholarly courses in contemporary art, among other things. I'm amazed you haven't heard of him! He's one of the foremost, the greatest teachers of our generation." I don't take this very seriously, since everything connected with Ingrid is either the foremost or the greatest or both in the world, according to Ingrid.

"That sounds interesting," I say.

"You must read Ed's essays on de Kooning and the first generation and their ties to the neo-expressionist movement." Ingrid speaks as if Ed weren't sitting right there. "You should do something about him at *Antics*, he's becoming more and more influential." She doesn't mention that my father also has written about de Kooning, his friend de Kooning.

"I imagine Elizabeth has inherited a few opinions about de Kooning herself," Ed says.

"De Kooning's use of brushstroke and depth *has* influenced *me*," Ingrid says. As she lectures on her work, Ed Lissner carefully quarters, cores, and peels an apple from the black lacquered fruit bowl and hands me a piece. It tastes cool and sweet, and I sip white wine and sit back and enjoy the afternoon moment, the astonishing winter light and the red clouds gathering in the west on the other side of the Hudson, the creamy cheese and the somehow reassuring sound of Ingrid talking about herself.

For a minute I wonder where Sebastian is, at the gallery or with his children, or arguing with Melissa, or *not* arguing with Melissa, and I wonder what he would think if he were here living *my* life, listening to Ingrid yak-yak and sharing an apple with a blocky academic.

As the light fades and the sky turns luminous pink, Ingrid switches on a soft bank of lights over our chairs. I get up to leave, and Ed Lissner walks me to the door. He has a shambling gait, and he wears jeans and an old tweed jacket with too short sleeves, and heavy lace-up boots.

"I'm sorry we didn't get to talk more," I say, because that seems polite. Ingrid has already kissed me goodbye, enfolding me in her silken caftan, enveloping me with the musky, cypressy scent of her perfume, and rushed off to answer her ringing telephone.

"Ingrid likes to talk, it's best to let her," he says, as if Ingrid's megalomania was one particularly charming aspect of her altogether charming personality. "We'll get to talk another time." He lets me out the door onto the long staircase and watches until I reach the bottom, where I turn and wave goodbye.

It's dark and the streetlights glare green as I approach Houston cars careen by on either side of the concrete divider. I remember that John Berkland was killed here, crossing the street for lunch on his way to Ballato's. The weekend is half over, one more day until I'll see Sebastian. Carefully I wait for a break in the traffic and walk quickly across, sprinting the last few feet to avoid a taxi bearing down on me from the east.

8 Tucking the Sunday paper under my left arm, I fit the key into the lock of my apartment door. It squeaks open on the white living room and the closed bedroom door, touched by the bands of sunlight which also imprison the kitchen counter. Something is wrong. As I step inside I notice the smell of roses. I've been gone ten minutes, but the equilibrium of silence in the rooms has been disturbed. My quick heartbeats tell me I should leave. You're supposed to get out right away if you come home and find the door open or anything different. I put the newspaper down and jump with fear when the uneasy stillness is shattered from behind me by Julie's laugh. Turning fast, I see that she's lying on the couch watching me. She must have picked the lock, I forgot that's one of her witchy skills.

"You scared me!" I'm half delighted and half terrified. My heart rate begins to settle down toward normal.

"It wasn't *hard*." Julie is still giggling. "You'd make a horrible spy! Don't I always come by for coffee on Sunday morning?"

Of course she does, and now I see that the kettle is spouting steam and that the coffee beans have been ground and spooned into the pot, and I *do* remember smelling coffee as I lumbered up the stairs with the paper. How could I have missed the significance of the rose perfume? Only Julie can smell like a summer garden at ten o'clock on a gray winter morning.

"You're so incorrigibly, adorably out of it!" Julie throws her arms in the air in affectionate exasperation. I consider giving her a stern, cautionary lecture on the inadvisability of picking locks and surprising people, but I know she'll just laugh and make me laugh, too, at my own prudishness. I pour the boiling water into the glass coffeepot, stir the grounds, and sit the metal plunger at the top while they steep. Julie stretches and walks around the counter into the kitchen. She's wearing a creamy silk man's pajama top tucked into jeans, and black ballet slippers. I push the plunger down against the grounds and breathe in the cloud of fragrance that billows from the top of the Melior.

"You look so fabulous in the morning, there's not a wrinkle!" Julie runs a fingernail along my cheek, and I feel transformed.

"Too much sleep," I say, taking down the mugs and pouring. When Sebastian makes coffee he always pours boiling water in first to warm the cups. I hand Julie the red mug and she lights on the sofa again, stretching out against the pillows like a sexy cat.

"Bad night?" I ask.

"Look, I've got something for us." Like a magician Julie produces a flat tinfoil package from the sofa cushions. "Have you got a mirror?"

Pouring the white powder on the glass side of the tortoise-shell hand mirror my father brought from Italy years ago, she forms four lines of cocaine with a gold razor blade she sometimes wears on a delicate chain around her neck.

"Where'd you get that?" I ask as Julie inhales two of the lines with a rolled-up ten-dollar bill and passes the mirror to me.

"Harvey West, the swinging professor," she says. "He tried bringing me flowers and then jewelry. He finally got wise." The powder feels cold and tingles inside my nostrils.

"How is old Harvey?" I'm already anticipating the feeling of lean power I get from Julie's drugs.

"Poor fellow, I guess you were right about him. He's getting boring."

"He lasted a long time—usually it's about two weeks."

"I thought he was different, my first real intellectual." Julie giggles and relaxes against the cushions. "He seemed so ethical. He didn't seem to care about money or status or any of that bullshit."

"What gave you that idea?"

"Maybe it was that he didn't want to sleep with me at first. He said I was dangerous, that I'd distract him from his work. He took his work so seriously!"

"He didn't want to sleep with you?"

"It was pretty impressive."

"How long did that last?"

Julie laughs and stretches her legs, shrugging so that the silk pajama top falls away from a frail, infinitely feminine collarbone. She yawns as if it's an old story—the story of how she had to maneuver yet another idiot male into doing her bidding. "When a man doesn't want to sleep with a woman there are always reasons: his wife, or work, or whatever. You never argue! Instead, you agree that he's absolutely right, that sleeping together would be the worst thing you could do."

"You co-opt their position."

"Pretty soon they begin to wonder if they *can* sleep with you."

"God, Julie, you're dangerous, you know that?"

Julie laughs again and dances out of the sofa cushions toward the window. "It's so easy," she says. "When I meet a man I just pretend that he's the first man I've ever seen and that everything about him is absolutely fascinating! I give him total attention. Whatever it takes. I act as if I'm just in from Mars and I can't wait to find out everything about this compelling, sexy earth-creature."

"So Harvey wasn't any different?" I sit down and unlace my sneakers, feeling superbly graceful and light. The socks leave wavy patterns on my pink feet and ankles. Julie rolls up the loose sleeves of her silk top and walks back across the room to the kitchen. She pours another cup of coffee from the pot and then, reaching into my cupboard for the bottle, she spikes it with Calvados. It's one of her Sunday-morning rituals.

"This is what they do in France for breakfast," she says. "Want some?"

"I'm feeling no pain," I say.

"Oh, come on, that stuff was just a warm-up." As Julie speaks the telephone on my desk begins to ring. I step toward it and then stop, looking at Julie.

"I told him you were my best friend," she says, and we both begin laughing. Harvey West has looked me up in the phone book. First he's called Julie's house and now he's looking for her here. If he can't find her, he'll take me. He'll want to talk about how incredible she is. He'll want reassurance.

"Should I answer?" I ask. Julie shakes her head.

"No, I don't want to talk to him anymore! Anyway, I'm here to see you!" After ten rings the telephone stops. A few seconds later when it starts to ring again we look at each other and laugh some more. I can't stop; it's as if someone were tickling me to the point of agony. I collapse in the armchair, still laughing and taking deep breaths. When the phone stops ringing I'm sobbing a little.

"Oh, God." Julie's voice is bubbling. "Do you think I'm a man-eater? That's what his friends say."

"You do what you do." I'm able to control my voice, but there's a dull ache in my stomach from the laughing. Now I feel like bursting into tears. "They're grownups, they have to take care of themselves."

"I keep wishing I could find one who could!"

"And if you did?" I'm calmer now, I feel numb.

"I'm not sure, I keep thinking that I *want* to be outwitted for once, that I want a man who makes *me* crazy instead of . . ."

"Could you let that happen? It's no fun, you know."

Julie's sitting on the arm of the sofa now, another cup of coffee, more Calvados. "Like Casey," she says.

"*Fuck* him." It was Julie who went to the clinic with me, who nursed me through the depression afterward, who waited with me for Casey to call.

"Do you ever think about him?"

"He's history!"

"But you . . ."

"It's classic, right?" I interrupt her. "The guy gets you pregnant and then he disappears. It's not the first time that's happened and it won't be the last. That's what's so great about you, with you *they're* the victims!"

"But he wanted the child."

"Are you defending that *shit*? You're the one who agreed that it would be crazy, that I'd be crazy to do that. You were right! For Christ's sake, Julie."

"It would have been crazy," she says, but I sit there floundering in anger and memories of Casey: Casey at the airport, Casey getting into his old car and driving away up Sullivan Street. Don't go, I would say, and when he left I would think I was going to die. Then the doctor's office. Lying there, the first sharp pain and then the feeling of something being scraped away, and then the bleeding. I have to ask you this, the doctor said: Are you sure?

"You're just trying to change the subject," I say.

"What?" Julie is distracted now; her attention has shifted and she walks over to my desk and flips through the *Antics* pasteups. My cover has to be done this week. "Do you know him? What a jerk!" She points to a spread we're doing on a big-deal art-world lawyer and his collection of Joel Shapiro's tiny furniture. I know that she doesn't expect an answer, some reverie has overtaken her. Maybe she's thinking about Harvey and the brief and shining moment when it seemed possible that he was the man she's looking for—the man who could resist her. Twenty telephone rings changed that. Maybe she's thinking about the Calvados bottle. She turns the gold rings on her fingers and stares out the window and I'm left with my rich and bitter memories of Casey and my sour sense of loss.

9 "I don't know why she brought it up." Dr. Rosen's leather chair squeaks as he leans back toward the beige wall. He's in a brown suit today with a drab knit tie and white shirt. His eyelids droop.

"I think it's because she doesn't like Sebastian."

"How does it make you feel?" He leans forward and suppresses a yawn.

"Or maybe she just wanted more Calvados."

"Do you think about Casey? Why does it bother you so much when Julie mentions him?"

"Of course I think about him. When someone dumps you, you never quite get over them. It's because you didn't control it; it doesn't mean anything. I'm thinking about him because I'm drawing that stupid cover, too, it's not just Julie."

"How do you feel about that?" Dr. Rosen folds his hands together and rocks backward.

"Confused. I mean, I decided not to be an artist; just because I can draw doesn't mean I want to be an artist."

"What if you tried?"

"No way!" I look past him to where cold raindrops make the roofs and water towers darken. This afternoon I'll see Sebastian and everything will be all right again. "That's what Casey used to ask me," I say.

"*Did* he dump you?" This time the yawn is wider, less suppressed.

"Isn't that what you call it when they don't call and they don't want to see you anymore and they don't answer your letters?"

"Umm-hmmm." Dr. Rosen leaves me to stew as he stares thoughtfully at the ceiling above my head. The plaster is coming away from the wall in fat, soft bubbles. His eyelids droop again.

"Well, isn't it," I say. "Why are you so sleepy?" Suddenly I'm furious at Dr. Rosen; I'd like to leap across his neutral wall-to-wall carpet and throttle him. Why can't he pay attention to me? Why is he falling asleep?

"What do you imagine?" he says, more alert now that we're talking about him.

"I imagine that you're bored, that you haven't had enough sleep, that I'm not interesting to you." I seethe. I'm not paying this man to fall asleep on me. I wonder if another, more interesting patient has exhausted him. Maybe he's sleeping with another patient, the cute, plump one who comes in before me and whom I sometimes see in the waiting room. Maybe that's why he's so tired.

"It may have nothing to do with you," he says, pushing his fingers together in the psychoanalytic steeple. "Do you think Julie's right?"

"I don't know and I don't care. It's over, what does it matter." Now I feel despair caress and embrace me. I couldn't keep Casey, I can't get Sebastian, I can't even hold my shrink!

"It may still be affecting you." He swivels and stares at me, trying to keep his eyes open. On the wall to his right is a Hokusai print of the wave; to his left another Japanese woodcut, mountain hawk and bridge. I see them through tears.

"We should look at why it's making you so angry," he says mildly. I notice a faint spot on the lapel of his suit. Does Dr. Rosen splatter when he eats?

"Of course I'm angry! I'm in love with someone who's jerking me around, the last guy I was in love with dumped me, and I can't even hold your interest!" I burst out. The tears leak down one cheek and I dab at them with the Kleenex from Dr. Rosen's ever-present box of Kleenex. Do his other patients cry?

"That's one way to see things." Dr. Rosen looks sleepy again. Andrew told me he once had a shrink who just put his head down on the desk and even began to snore while he talked.

Is it the family? Is there something deeply, inherently boring about our story?

"You look sleepy again," I say.

"I may be sleepy, but it may have absolutely nothing to do with you," he says, leaning forward again. "Why do you assume that you're causing everything that happens?"

"It seems that way sometimes," I say.

"Or maybe you choose people who allow it to seem that way." Dr. Rosen glances at the clock now and turns slightly in his chair toward the telephone. I can see that our time is almost up and that he has calls to make, important calls.

"How was the shrink?" Sebastian asks.

"Bored," I say, laughing as if this were funny. Sebastian's looking over my shoulder at the cover drawings. I didn't hear him come up the stairs.

"With you? Impossible! Here." He hands me a glass of white wine which he's brought from the kitchen.

"We were talking about you, actually," I lie.

"Oh well, then . . ." Sebastian puts a hand on my shoulder. "Those drawings look interesting," he says. He can't help himself. There's not a picture in the world that Sebastian can resist analyzing.

"Have a look." I spread them out on the table. He picks up the most finished one, a Golden Gate Bridge in a surreal, foreshortened perspective, and scrutinizes it with the same narrowing of the eye that I have seen him bring to a Rauschenberg sketch or a Johns drawing.

When Sebastian looks at a painting or drawing it gets his complete soul; it's as if he were making love to it. If it's small enough he takes it gently off the wall or the easel and brings it close to his face, almost touching it, as if he wanted to smell it and graze the smooth surface with his lips. Slowly he moves it back and forth a few inches from his eyes, watching for each pencil or brushstroke as if it might hold a clue, or with old paintings as if he could see right through the paint and across the years to the artist's intention. In galleries or museums he stands back from a picture and slowly moves toward it until he's standing a hand's breadth away. During these moments he's totally lost. I have the feeling then that nothing can bring him back to this world, to the windows and the park and to Madison Avenue outside, to the chairs or the adulatory gallery assistants or the possibility of a good lunch. He moves slowly back and forth, stalking, as if the picture might shift or change if he watches closely enough.

"You can certainly draw, Elizabeth," he says, putting my sketches back down. "Since when have you been doing pictures like this?"

"Never. I'm not, it's just that the photographs for the cover didn't work and Grimy was desperate." Sebastian looks around my tiny studio with new interest, taking in the stacks of old paintings and the rolls of canvas and paper on the rickety shelves. "Come here," he says.

Sex with Sebastian is definitely a mind-altering substance. I can feel my hyperactive brain shutting down as we kiss and begin to undress. Dr. Rosen, Julie, my cover sketches all recede into a haze as my physical need takes over. Soon the only important thing, the only thing in the world at all, is to be under Sebastian, in bed with Sebastian, to have Sebastian inside me pushing against me, running his hands over me, building my desire until it explodes irresistibly into waves of feeling.

"This is heaven," Sebastian murmurs afterward, as we lie there. In a while he gets up and takes our glasses into the kitchen to pour more wine. He comes back and props himself against the pillows with a full glass. I reach over and stroke his smooth stomach.

"Melissa and I had a bad fight last night, I told her every-thing," he says.

"What!" I jump and wine spills on Sebastian and the sheets.

"Elizabeth! what a klutz!"

"Why didn't you tell me right away? What happened?" I settle myself away from the wet spots.

"She confronted me again, she's been brooding since that night at the Whitney. She's furious. She's had a few consultations with a lawyer, I guess."

"What does she say?"

"If I won't give you up, she wants a divorce. She can't live this way."

"It's not as if she treats you so well." I'm terrified. What if Sebastian announces that, therefore, he has decided he must give me up?

"She doesn't want the children to have to go through the anger and bitterness of us divorcing. I don't blame her."

"That's just an excuse."

"You wouldn't say that if you had children."

"Oh, excuse *me*!" But Sebastian doesn't notice my sarcasm.

"She thinks I'm just going through a mid-life crisis, that it's some kind of arrested adolescence. She has a lot of theories."

"That doesn't sound like love."

"She can love me and still be so angry that it sounds as though she hates me, can't you understand that? If our marriage ends it would be the end of her life in a way; she's not like you, she doesn't have anything else."

"It was easier not to. She *could* have."

"I didn't want her to! I wanted her to live my life. Now that I've changed my mind, why should she have to adjust?"

"That's what happens, people change, other people have to adjust."

"She just stood there last night in tears, asking, How can you just have stopped loving me like that? How can you just stop loving someone? It was awful." Sebastian pulls the sheet taut around his body.

"Doesn't she know anyone else this has happened to? It's an old, old story."

"I guess she never thought . . . Anyway, then she blew up and they served me the papers at the gallery this morning, so maybe she knew all along." Sebastian's voice dips. It sounds as if the end of his marriage—if this *is* the end of his marriage—

is as bad for him as it is for Melissa. I can feel anger and depression building walls around me. I didn't ask for this. It was *his* bright idea.

"I'll take care of you," I say, reaching over to hug his rigid form before it's too late and I let my own feelings create a pressure that I can't control. "Don't worry."

"I can't help it," he says. He doesn't move.

"It's hard, I know it's hard, baby," I say, concentrating on the challenge of making him feel better. I kiss him gently on the forehead.

"It seems to be happening so fast. I feel as if my life has suddenly gone out of control."

"It takes a lot of courage, what you're doing is very hard," I say, stroking his hair back from his face. "It'll take you a long time to work all this out." I'd like to kill him.

"Thank God I have you," he says.

10

I kneel on the wide boards and pull canvas over the wooden stretchers with my old pliers, carefully balancing my weight. If it's too tight, it rips; if it's too loose, it sags. I haven't painted for months and the San Francisco sketches are still on my table. To do one thing completely, I have to do another thing at the same time. I'm jamming the staple gun against the canvas when the doorbell rings.

"Right down," I call out the window, hoping Karen can hear me. When I get there, sucking my finger from a splinter, she's staring down the street toward Bleecker, leaning against the iron railings with her yellow hair streaming out over a denim jacket. Maybe because of Andrew, I always forget how pretty Karen is.

"Ready?" She smiles her dimply smile. Karen has creamy skin and a face like a porcelain cherub. She called yesterday to say she had to visit an East Village gallery because she's doing a piece on appropriation art, and she asked me to go with her. I took this as an attempt to salvage what was left of our friendship after her last breakup with Andrew, and I said yes. As we swing up the street and cross Bleecker Street together, I have a flash of resentment at my brother.

It's the February thaw and old people are sitting on the benches in Washington Square with their faces turned toward the warm sun. On the sidewalk outside Cooper Union, vendors in black preside over a long flea market of clothes and junk, hawking and bargaining. On the corner of St. Marks Place four men and a girl are singing *a capella* oldies from the sixties.

Anthea Riley's new gallery is in a ruined block, the buildings around it are crumbling. A bag lady pulling two shopping carts of worldly goods has stopped to smoke a butt on a tire in one of the vacant lots across the street, where rusting refrigerators are shaded by the spindly locust trees that grow wherever there's a New York inch of topsoil.

Inside, through a heavy metal fire door bolted into the brick, there's a flat cement floor and skylit space where Riley has created half a dozen instant careers in the past two years. This month she's showing Rake Martins, a hot twenty-five-year-old Yale MFA who's one of the leaders of "appropriation art." When Picasso said art is piracy, he probably didn't mean this. Martins copies a famous painting in every detail, signs it, and shows it as his work. The idea started with Marcel Duchamp, with Duchamp's ready-mades, and with Duchamp's revolutionary ideas about the nature of originality.

Rake Martins talks about his debt to Duchamp, but the popularity of appropriation art has nothing to do with revolutionary ideas about anything. Most of the collectors who buy a Martins painting for $30,000 and up don't even know who Duchamp was. They like the work because they get the familiarity and vouched-for quality of a contemporary masterpiece, combined with the satisfaction of being avant-garde.

Still, as I walk through the entryway into the big room I'm surprised by the sheer beauty of the work against white stucco walls. There are Léger and Picasso and Rothko; so what if they're rip-offs? The eight paintings stand out like windows into another world. There's a Stella protractor, a George Mallet, and the wild splash of a small de Kooning. It doesn't matter that they're copies, it only matters that they're beautiful.

A child's high-pitched scream intrudes on the silence and Neddy Dearing appears at the entrance of the gallery, his long gray hair standing up on end, his stooped body pushing a stroller overflowing with his protesting son.

"I don't *want* to make a deal!" the child shrieks, crumbling a street pretzel in one sweaty fist.

"Behold," Karen whispers, "the foremost art critic of our generation. The fruits of marriage to a younger woman." She sounds bitter. I know how much Karen wants a child. Dearing fumbles with the plastic buckles, which barely restrain the struggling child. When they finally open, the boy pops out of confinement and caroms across the room, coming within inches of the "Stella." Dearing wrestles to fold the stroller, which looks like a stubborn metal-and-canvas bird. His foot gets caught in the wheels and then his hand; as it folds, a crumbled cookie drops to the floor along with a dented toy truck and a half-empty bottle of juice. A sleek gallery assistant appears from the tiny inner office with a scowl. She seems about to eject Dearing and son, but as I watch she recognizes him and changes course, welcoming him with a toothy smile and an English-accented invitation to park the stroller in the office, as if nothing was more thrilling for a young gallery owner than an afternoon visit from Dennis the Menace and his hen-pecked dad.

"Let's walk over to Gray Anderson's," I say, when we both drift toward the door. "Ingrid's show is still up, she'll probably be there." Karen moves with me out into the fading afternoon light.

"It's great to see you again," she says as we head into the traffic at Cooper Square.

"I can't help liking those paintings," I say. Andrew is just below the surface of Karen's voice and I don't want to talk about him. "They aren't real Rothkos or Stellas, but there's something pleasing . . ."

"But they *aren't* Rothkos, that's exactly it!" Karen's vehemence seems more a response to my refusal to discuss Andrew than the paintings. "Rothko was a painter, a man who lived and died by it. This guy is a salesman, an art student with a great producer. Without the lighting and the viewer's built-in associations with the work, those paintings would be nothing. They have no meaning!" Karen's face is flushed. I guide her out of the way of a taxi speeding down Mercer Street. The cab screeches to a halt. Karen doesn't seem to notice. It's getting dark and the neon lights of restaurants and stores are flashing on around us.

"But it's still seductive." Karen writes about art, so she knows what she's talking about. Still, her passion surprises me. We're walking across Washington Square toward Houston Street. It's five o'clock—the hour when everyone walks their dogs. About forty spotted ones, and black and brown and white ones, small ones and big ones play and tumble in a furry knot near the arch.

"But good art isn't supposed to be seductive," Karen says. "It's supposed to be visionary. I don't think anyone expects enough. Even the pieces I write—if they're competent and they don't rock the boat, that's as good as it gets. Art should change things, shouldn't it? It seems as if all anyone wants anymore is pleasure."

"Pleasure and prettiness." I wonder if she's referring to Andrew again. Is pleasure all he wants? Maybe Karen is right. I remember Ingrid's furious story about a trustee of the Museum of Modern Art who asked her to do a pale peach painting because her decorator had chosen pale peach as the color for her living room.

"There's a lot of talk about art being more fashionable than visionary these days," Karen says. "You can't blame them, I guess. After abstract expressionism and neo-expressionism and neo-geo and pattern painting and the Italians and the Germans and neo-realism and postmodernism, people are too beaten up to think. They're happy if art isn't offensive. If it's not someone's genitals, or a nude portrait of the painter's male lover, or some realistic depiction of childhood sex, they're so relieved! If they can hang it on their walls and not feel embarrassed when their friends come for dinner, they'll buy it!"

"Imagine him appropriating George Mallet," I say as we wait to cross Houston Street.

"Sebastian's friend." Karen's voice twists ironically.

"He *was* a friend." I step into the street in front of Karen.

"A profitable friend." We stand on the island in the middle of Houston, with cars whizzing by on both sides. "I hear the Mallet children are threatening to sue," Karen says.

"They made millions," I say. "Sebastian helped."

"At least you and Sebastian are together," Karen says. Poor

Karen, mourning a man who never thinks about her. She should be more like Julie. Julie lives in a simpler world. Either she has complete control over a man or she is working *toward* that most desirable of goals. It's men versus women with her. She takes no prisoners.

Upstairs in the gallery rooms, a dozen people mill in front of Ingrid's splashy paintings. They're all sold, I know. When Gray Anderson arranges a show, he lines up a few key collectors beforehand. The paintings are sold right out of the studio. Only a failure has paintings still for sale on opening night—and Gray Anderson doesn't show failures.

Ingrid is on a roll. Her passionate conviction in her own genius is contagious. On the walls the vigor of her colors projects toward the spectators and draws them in. I still don't like the pictures, any more than I did when I saw them in her studio, any more than when I looked at them on opening night, but I envy their confident, large scale.

"Strong paintings." Karen seems slightly stunned by Ingrid's overpowering energy. Over her shoulder I see Ed Lissner in the next room, talking to a woman with lots of dark frizzy hair.

"They're so certain, so sure of themselves," I say. "I don't know why that bothers me."

"Confidence is the genius of the eighties," Karen says.

"Everyone's shell-shocked," I say. "Look what's happened in thirty years. First they all thought ab ex was a joke, then they all thought Rauschenberg was a joke. He hung his bed on the wall! He put a tire around a goat! Now that goat is worth a fortune. Then they all thought pop art was a joke. No one knows what to think."

"Not knowing what to think is fine. Accepting what other people tell you to think is the problem."

We've wandered into the next room and I introduce Ed Lissner to Karen, and Ed introduces me to the dark-haired woman—Sue Stanley.

"Sue has a gallery in California," Ed says. "She's looking for space in New York."

"It's a jungle," I say. She laughs; her face crinkles up around her eyes in a friendly way.

"This is forceful work," she says, gesturing at the painting in front of her. "But I'd have trouble selling it out there."

"It's loft painting," Ed says. "You need huge blank walls for this work. In San Francisco everyone lives in houses. There's nowhere to put something like this." I guiltily savor secret gratification at hearing Ingrid criticized, if only for the size of her work.

"It's not just that, life is calmer out there. There's less market for what's fashionable." She looks over at me, where I'm wondering if Patrick Casey's disdain for fashionable things was just a Northern California character trait. "Of course your father is the exception that proves the rule," she says. "Those pictures . . . one of the truly great painters." I decide that I don't like Sue Stanley.

"All an exception proves is that the rule was wrong in the first place," I say.

"Clever, clever," Karen says. Ed Lissner is laughing.

11 "You hear about the dealers hurting, but then you go to Gray Anderson's," Ed Lissner says. We've left Karen in a phone booth on Prince Street. She says she has to call the magazine; I hope she's not calling Andrew.

"The auction houses are hurting them."

"That could be true."

"The auction houses are like banks now: they can lend money, they can advance it on a collection, they can reach all kinds of customers, people a normal dealer can't just call."

"There are other reasons that the dealers are at war with the auction houses, although you're right."

"Like what?" I remember Sebastian's frequent complaints about the auction houses and the way they've pirated away sales from the dealers.

"They're regulated now. They've all been investigated by the Consumer Affairs people, so it's much less likely that they'll cheat."

"Come on! They set reserves, they try to charge half of what a collection brings over the reserve, they bid in-house. I hear one of the brass at Sotheby's bought the two best pictures out of the Gould sale himself! Didn't he have to return one?"

"I heard that, too, but that doesn't alter the collector's perception. At an auction they see it with their own eyes—a picture goes on the block, someone bids a price, it gets knocked down. Often they even know who bought it! When they sell through a dealer they know nothing—only what the dealer wants to tell them."

"The dealer has to protect his sources, too. They don't have the resources of a big auction house behind them," I say.

We're walking slowly up Sullivan Street. I dawdle because I'm not sure if I want to invite Ed Lissner up.

"They may be protecting other things, too, although . . . Why didn't you like Sue Stanley?" Ed Lissner asks.

"I *did*, it's just that I'm not thrilled when people talk about my father as if he were some kind of dead saint."

"You can't blame people for admiring him."

"I guess not. It just makes me uncomfortable; it's as if I'm obligated to worship with them."

"Or else be a spoilsport?"

"That's it. He wasn't exactly a perfect father, although he may be a perfect painter."

"And you never wanted to be a painter?" Ed Lissner has slowed his footsteps to match mine. Going this slowly makes me cold and I shiver.

"You're cold." He gives me a warming squeeze with his big arm and hand.

"I wasn't good enough," I say, laughing to ease my movement away from him.

"What made you think that?" Now Ed Lissner has stopped completely and turned to look at me.

"It wasn't just something *I* thought," I say.

"It's quite a sweeping judgment for a talented young woman to make, I'd say." He sounds as if he is talking about someone else, a student. "Not good enough."

"I'm a good draftsman, I'm good at design, that's what I like doing. It's *real*. It's *useful*. I don't want to be an artist. I hate all that artist shit! All that blah blah blah about creativity and facing the inner self and channeling and the Muse; it's all vague and pretentious. People get so pompous about their inner lives! And most of them can't even draw."

"So you'd rather not try."

"I'd rather be honest and realistic. I'd rather not join the ranks of fervent, useless, aspiring creative artists." I hate Ed Lissner for his smug questions. I will definitely not invite him up.

"You were very young."

"Where do you live?" I ask. We're standing in front of my house.

Ed Lissner laughs. "Okay, sorry if I got didactic, we can change the subject. I have an apartment over near the library; the university rents it to me."

"Of course!" I hit my forehead with the heel of my hand in mock remorse. "Of course, Ingrid said you teach at NYU." I dimly remember someone else, too, talking about Ed Lissner's fire and his dedication and his refusal to become a curator because of his zeal for scholarship.

"One of the foremost minds of our generation," he says. "How could you forget?"

"That's right." I laugh.

"So," he blurts out as I get ready to shake hands and say good night, "are you married, or what?" He leans his square body against a parked car.

"No, but I'm in love with someone who is."

"You like married men? I should have stayed married?"

I smile to acknowledge the compliment. I'm cold and I have to pee and I can't wait to curl up in one of Julie's chairs with a hot cup of tea and tell her about my latest conquest. To pass the time I decide to pretend that Ed Lissner is the first man I've ever met; that I'm from another planet and that everything he says and does is fascinating.

"What was your marriage like?" I say.

"Is this guy the first man you've been in love with?"

"No." I remember the last time I saw Casey at the airport. I'll call you, I said. I'll see you soon. He didn't answer. He kissed me goodbye quickly and stepped into the elevator, his face a sad moon eclipsed by the sliding silver door. I remember the hissing sound of the elevator being moved down the shaft, and my sharp relief and my sharp regret.

"You don't want to talk about it?"

"Aaaargh." I wrinkle my nose. "It's too cold to talk about anything. Maybe another time."

"Let's have lunch or something." Ed Lissner straightens his big body and puts out his hand.

"Sure." I shake hands with him, braced for him to make a move, but he doesn't. I turn into my doorway as he shambles off. When he disappears around the corner of Bleecker Street I dart down the block to Julie's.

"Is Mrs. Lowe at home?" I ask Bonita. The warmth inside Julie's door feels delicious. My hands begin to tingle as they unfreeze.

"Yes, Missus." Bonita stands back to let me pass and withdraws into the kitchen. I'm still shivering as I step into the downstairs hall. Julie's house was decorated by Ronald Winthrop to look like an English country cottage; the walls are pale blue with green moldings which are hung with gold-framed paintings of sexy shepherdesses and rose gardens in afternoon light.

Upstairs, Samantha's door is closed, she spends the weekends with her father, and as I approach Julie's room I expect to hear her voice chattering away on the phone. She's lying propped against the piles of lace and eyelet pillows at the carved wooden head of the big bed. Julie often receives visitors in her bedroom, but tonight even the sumptuous surroundings and the flattering lamplight can't disguise the stark white of her face as she lies there asleep.

"Julie?" I whisper from the door. If she's sound asleep, I don't want to wake her. I walk closer to the bed and see that her body is askew, ungracefully jackknifed under the covers. On the bedside table a bottle of poire brandy squats next to her collection of pills and telephones. As I watch, her whole body shivers as if some internal vibration is shaking it. Her arms and legs heave like a rag doll's.

"Julie?" I ask louder. The bottles of pills look familiar—vitamins, Percodan for her bad back and hangovers, the special Tylenol, the Halcion for sleeping. She shifts slightly and the shivering begins again.

"Julie!" I reach out and grab her delicate shoulder. The shaking stops but her mouth falls slightly open; her breathing is rapid and shallow.

"Julie, for God's sake!" This time she opens her eyes.

"What?" she mouths, but no sound emerges. For a moment I see fear in her eyes. "What's the matter?" Her voice is a hoarse grate of air. "What is it?" A tinge of color brushes her cheeks.

"Were you asleep?" I ask, incredulous.

"Obviously." Julie pushes herself up against the pillows. "I just lay down to take a nap. What's the big deal? God, you scared me with that look on your face!" Now her body is upright, her arms and legs entrancingly arranged, her pallor suggesting frailty instead of death.

"I couldn't wake you up," I say.

"You certainly did wake me up! Do you want some coffee? Bonita!" she calls in the direction of the stairs. I stare across her at the pastoral scene on the wall next to the window: a man in knee breeches kneels to take the hand of a woman in full skirts.

"Sit down, for heaven's sake, you're making me nervous," Julie says. I sink into one of the blue chairs as Bonita brings a silver tray with coffee cups clinking into the room. Julie pours me a cup. I notice that her hands are still shaky. I sit back and make funny stories out of Ed Lissner's clumsy show of interest. Julie smiles and laughs, but she seems exhausted. As I talk she leans back and her eyes close. When I laugh, she opens them and laughs with me.

"I'm sorry if I scared you," she says when I get up to leave. "My back has been killing me, and I'm always sad when Samantha goes off. Maybe I overdid it with the brandy; forgive me for being so grouchy."

"Oh, no big deal," I say. "I probably should have let you sleep."

"Don't be a goose! I needed to talk to you. I was missing Samantha and now I feel a lot better." Julie is her old, teasing self. "And I *had* to hear about your latest conquest!" As I leave, Bonita shuts and bolts the door behind me. A February wind is pushing down the street and around the corner from the river where the pavement ends and rotting piers jut out into the dangerous, opaque Hudson currents. The thaw is over. The cold stays with me even when I'm back at home, wrapped in a blanket and drinking hot tea. Outside my window the trees rattle their icy branches.

12 My cab gets mired in the garment-district traffic on Sixth Avenue, and I sit there staring happily out the grimy window at the rush-hour crowds, messengers on bicycles, delivery boys in blue jackets, stock kids pushing racks of plastic-covered summer dresses through the cold March air, the rumpled weary drones of fashion in their cloth coats, and an occasional Queen Bee dressed in fur and the crisp long skirt and short jacket of the moment. In a doorway, a white man in tight jeans and a leather jacket passes money to a black man in a knitted green, black, and red beanie. A truck pulls up to the sidewalk at Thirty-second Street, and one of the delivery boys loads two racks of clothes—these are the stolen sweaters and dresses that street vendors will be selling uptown tomorrow. The rented truck peels off into downtown traffic. Two men in matching red duffel coats hold hands as they walk into a coffee shop; one is thin and losing his hair, his face strained by disease. Cars honk, cabbies scream obscenities, their voices making clouds of mist in the cold air; buses belch carcinogenic fumes, but I don't care. I stretch my legs forward and admire their shape and my new patent-leather pumps. Winter is ending at last; there's still light in the sky as we speed through the park. God's in his heaven, all's right with the world. Sebastian has moved out of his apartment, and he's living at the Stanhope.

I sail triumphantly through the hotel lobby and past the front desk to the elevator. I love hotels, with their perfect combination of anonymity and service. Everything is done for you. Your wishes are granted. As the elevator ascends I imagine the celebration we'll have tonight, champagne and sex in the erotic strangeness of hotel sheets. It's been a year and a half since I met Sebastian, maybe now we will get on with our life together.

At the door of his room, I take off one of my pumps and knock out Shave and a haircut, two bits! with the heel. After a few minutes, I knock again. Finally I hear a rustling sound and the door being unlocked from inside. Instead of his usual English suit, or a casual blue blazer and flannels, or his country-gentleman cabled cashmere and cords, Sebastian is wearing a white undershirt and baggy chinos. His neck looks scrawny without a collar, and his eyes are crusty and red as if he has just been asleep.

"Were you asleep?" I reach up and kiss him.

"No, I'm just trying to get things organized. It's a bit difficult, working out of a hotel room." He walks toward the bed, where piles of paper and slides cover the flower-patterned spread. His jacket, flannels, and a crumpled dress shirt are thrown over a chair near the closed curtains.

I step past him and pull a cord at the edge of the heavy flowered fabric; the curtains creak open and radiant evening light streams into the cluttered room. Outside, I can see the corner of a brick apartment building and a sliver of the trees in Central Park.

"I guess this is a New York room with a view," I say. Sebastian doesn't answer. He sits on the bed absorbed in sorting papers while I hang up his jacket and pants, put his shoes away in the closet, and cram his dirty shirt into the metal laundry hamper on the bathroom wall. Above the bed hang two faded prints of men playing polo. As I put his suitcase away on the closet floor I notice that he has brought only one other suit and two clean shirts from home. When I've picked up, I call room service and order caviar and champagne to go with it, but Sebastian still doesn't look up from a catalogue which he appears to be matching with slides from a portfolio. By the time the waiter has set up the round table with the white tablecloth, chilled champagne flutes, and caviar in a silver dish propped in a glass dish of shaved ice, his ceremony seems absurd. Sebastian studies catalogues as the waiter pops

the cork and invites me to taste. I sip and nod; he gently decants
the champagne into the glasses.

"Sebastian, what's the matter?"

"What?" He's buried in a catalogue. The door clicks shut
behind the waiter.

"I said, What's the matter?"

Sebastian looks up as if he's just noticed that he's not alone.
"Oh." He shrugs. "Hotels can get pretty grim sometimes." A
muscle twitches at the side of his cheek.

"This isn't so bad, champagne, sunlight, the woman you
love . . . what's bothering you?"

"Nothing," he says. I curl my body around his slumped
back on the unmade bed and kiss his neck.

"I'm not letting you up until you talk!" I whisper. He doesn't
move as I plant little kisses around his ears. "You might as
well give in."

"Elizabeth!" He stands abruptly, throwing me against the
padded headboard. "Please! I have to work."

"You can work later, this is playtime; have a drink."

"There isn't going to be any playtime."

"Oh, I see, life is real! life is earnest!"

"It *is* real. Not everything is a game as you sometimes seem
to think. I can't just leave my wife and children in the lurch
and then cat around as if I didn't have a care in the world."

"In the lurch! I thought they were in their apartment." He
doesn't smile. "Sebastian, you haven't left your children.
You're going to see them all the time, as much as they want
to see you. You'll see them more now! You've had the courage
to end a bad marriage, a marriage that wasn't good for anyone."

"*They* thought it was fine."

"They're children, they don't know what you know. This
will be better than fine, it's just a hard, hard adjustment."

"I hope so." Sebastian heaves himself off the bed and collapses into the chair, sitting on a black sock and his tie, which
I failed to hang up.

"It's one of the hardest things anyone ever does, but it's not
as if you haven't thought about it. Children do manage and

thrive in these situations," I say. He needs Intensive Care.
"*You* know it's not good for kids to live in a household where
there's so much anger and disconnection. This is a terrible
moment, but you did the right thing. Can't you trust your
own judgment?"

"It's not as if I didn't think about it."

"That's right! It's something you've been agonizing over for
months. You've talked with Melissa, you've seen the psychi-
atrists, you've done everything you could, you've really tried
to make it work. It's not some kind of self-indulgent whim!"
I slide down to the floor and hug his knee.

"Baby, don't punish yourself," I say. "You're doing the best
you can."

"I feel so guilty, Melissa really got to me this afternoon.
Sasha's been crying and Natasha doesn't understand what's
happened and keeps asking when I'm coming home . . ." His
voice breaks.

"Poor Sebastian, it's so hard." I stand up and gently massage
his shoulders. The muscles at the back of his neck feel like
rocks and I roll them under his skin. "It's awful now, but it'll
be okay, they'll be better than okay. You're still their father
and you always will be. You really love them. Separations
happen all the time, their friends at school have probably
already been through this. Melissa's so angry, of course she's
making it sound as bad as she can."

"That's true. It's not as if they're losing me. We probably
had the last intact marriage in Natty's class. Mmmm, that feels
good." I lower my circling hands, pushing Sebastian's muscles
in figure eights along his spine and leaning him forward so
that I can reach his lower back. His wedding ring flashes on
his left hand as he reaches around to pull me forward. He
throws me down on the cataglogues and slides which cover
the bed, pushes up my skirt, and pins down my shoulders with
his hands.

"You bitch!" He kisses me so hard that our teeth grate. "You
have really messed me up!" He sounds half fond, half furious

as he roughly pushes my legs apart with his knees and pulls open the front of my shirt.

"Sebastian, wait!" His response is to take my wrists in one hand and hold them above my head while he yanks off the rest of my clothes with the other. He's much stronger than I expected; Sebastian's always been such a gentleman. Once, I had a boyfriend who used to hit me. Every now and then we'd get into a fight and soon we'd be screaming and hissing, and then he'd slap me hard across the face with the flat of his hand. I was always secretly glad when this happened. When he hit me, the fight was over and I had won. The black eye I had the next morning was a badge of my righteousness and his brutality. Until it faded, he treated me like a princess. I used to tell my parents I'd walked into a door, or opened a cupboard too fast. They never asked any questions.

Now Sebastian fucks me as if I'm not there, pushing his body against mine with animal grunts until he comes and falls asleep on top of me. Afterward, in the tangle of hotel sheets, I wait until his breathing is regular and heavy. At first I don't dare move, but then I slide out from underneath him, slip quietly out of bed, and reach for the flat champagne.

13 One of the production guys slaps stats of the May cover on my desk. The drawing of San Francisco looks flippant and insubstantial to me now, although there was a moment when I liked it well enough to turn it in.

"It came out well, don't you think?" Judith Grimes-Gurewitz is looking over at my desk. Her voice is proprietary, as if *she* had spent nights sweating over the cover instead of me. "I'm writing the editor's note on you. Anything in particular you want me to say?"

"What did you have in mind?" My name at the bottom of the cover drawing looks huge. I wish I had a signature that no one could decipher. I wish I were married and had another name.

"You know, promising young talent, artistic dynasty, your father's mantle; people love that stuff."

"Yuck," I say.

"It's very flattering, Elizabeth. A lot of young artists would kill to do a cover for me; this kind of attention can really help."

"I'm not an artist."

"Well, you could have fooled me." Grimy is getting impatient. She looks back across the room to where her assistant has a telephone against each ear.

"I want to take my name off the drawing, and I don't want to be mentioned in the editor's note, okay?"

"That's crazy!" For a moment her attention snaps back to me, then wavers. Her assistant is signaling wildly from across the room.

"It's what I want. Use the drawing, but just take off the signature, okay?"

"If that's what you want. Jesus Christ!" Grimy lets me know
what she thinks of my reticence as she hurries off. After everyone else has left the office I sit at my desk. I don't want to be
an artist. I certainly don't want to be hailed as the talented
daughter of the great Fairfax Cole. As I put on my sweater
and sling my black leather bag, my warring feelings segue into
a kind of blank calm which persists as I walk uptown through
SoHo and across Houston Street and turn the corner toward
home. Nothing seems quite real. I wonder if I am talented,
or if the drawing was a fluke. Maybe it's no good at all, but
Grimy just wants to play the artistic dynasty angle. How will
I ever know? I cross Sullivan Street. It occurs to me that
Sebastian will probably want me to move in somewhere with
him, up to Park Avenue or down to some perfect loft space,
and I feel a wave of premature nostalgia for my pretty house
and my street with its row of brick fronts and gardens in the
back and the men lounging in front of the American Legion
post and the tourists buying tickets to *The Fantasticks*, and my
little apartment overflowing with my sentimental mementos.
It's a dump, but it's my dump.

As I approach my door, I see that someone is standing and
waiting for me outside in the gathering darkness.

"What a surprise!" I kiss my brother Andrew. "What made
you think I'd be coming home just now?"

"Just a hunch."

"Nice for me."

"I was standing here in the twilight, drinking in the excep-
tional beauty of your street, the trees just budding, the Ed-
wardian detail, the song of the turtle," he says.

"I was thinking the same thing. I was feeling sad about
having to leave."

"Look at the way it curves slightly to the west, the smooth
architectural transition to the commercialism of Bleecker
Street, the superb scale of the houses." Andrew ignores my
bombshell.

"I thought you hated the Village. What's gotten into you?"

"Are you going to give me shit, or do I get invited upstairs?"

We turn and walk through the big front door and up the flights of inner stairs.

"What brings you down here?" I ask idly as I grind the coffee beans and heat the water.

"I had an interesting lunch."

"Business downtown?" I pour water into the grounds and stir them, then fill up the pot with steaming water. "Have you seen Karen?" I ask. "How is she?"

"Better, I guess, recovering from the cruel depredations inflicted on her frail person by this brute."

"I don't think that's funny." I plunge the top of the pot down through the water and coffee bubbles up through the mesh netting.

"Everyone has to take responsibility for themselves, Lizzie. At least that's what my shrink says. *You* believe that. I can't feel guilty about Karen, she could have left anytime."

"But she loved you."

"Not enough to listen to me."

"Yeah, yeah, okay. *You* didn't have to comfort her afterward."

"Add to the list of my crimes! Don't you want to know who I had lunch with?"

"Henry Kissinger."

"No, but someone short and powerful." He smiles and gazes out the window into the romantic late-evening light.

"Dr. Ruth?"

"No."

"I give up; do you want coffee or not?"

"A friend of yours."

"Sebastian. You wanted to ask what his intentions were."

Andrew flushes and laughs; he's in a wonderful mood, the kind of generous euphoria I remember from before he went to college, before he became Mr. Big Shot. "No, a woman."

"Not Ingrid," I say, "and not Karen . . ." But suddenly I know exactly who Andrew had lunch with and why he ended up looking dreamy and rhapsodic on my doorstep.

"Oh shit," I say.

"That's the way you talk about your closest friend?"

"Did she call you or did you call her?"

"At the Whitney opening, she asked me about finding a lawyer for some of Samantha's trust problems. I forgot all about it, but yesterday I was sending my evening clothes to the cleaner and found the slip of paper with her number."

"And she just happened to be free for a long lunch?"

"What's the matter with you? She thinks *you're* wonderful. We spent hours talking about how terrific you are, for God's sake."

"It's just that, Andrew, please, please, please don't fall in love with Julie!" The minute I say this, I know I've made a bad mistake.

"Don't worry. Jesus! I'm not about to fall in love with anyone. Who would want me anyway, considering the ranks of keening females bearing witness to my evil nature?"

"No one ever said you have an evil nature! I didn't mean to defend Karen, you're right, she was responsible too, but Julie! You don't know . . ."

"You are overreacting, we just had lunch! I took her around to Da Silvano and then we walked back and had coffee in her garden. She's a very unusual woman, very quick; she drinks too much and flirts too much. I think I can help her with some legal problems, her child-support provisions are a joke."

"There were reasons." I vividly imagine the high of the stroll in early spring weather back to Julie's and the charm of coffee served in her English garden, her long skirt spread out against a wooden chair, the wings of her dark hair framing a laugh.

"Are you hinting at some dark past, or are you calling your best friend a crook?"

"No, she's a witch. I love her and she's a witch. I'm sorry, Andrew." I sit down, take a sip of the cooling coffee, and will myself to become rational. "I'm hyper today, I had a fight with Grimy and Sebastian's in some crisis up at the Stanhope. He's moved out. I'm just tired. What about Harvey West? I guess that's over, then."

"Harvey West?" A shadow crosses my brother's handsome face. He's already jealous of her past! "Is that someone I know?"

"Listen, bro, I didn't mean to jump all over you." Julie has him, I might as well be nice about it. "I'm pretty wound up, Sebastian's totally freaking out."

"Because he's left home? It was about time."

"It's the guilt, and Melissa doesn't help."

"That'll pass," Andrew says reassuringly, with an echo of Julie's confidence. "You'll be living with him before you know it. I'm more worried about how you'll fare as Mrs. Sebastian Smith. You're not exactly the handmaiden type."

"What makes you think Sebastian needs a handmaiden?"

"What makes *you* think I could fall under the spell of a witch like Julie Lowe?" I laugh, Andrew laughs, and we're friends again.

"Could you pass the broccoli, Mummy. I drew the cover of the May issue," I say. "The editor wanted to write the editor's note about me, or really about me and you, Daddy." A fire crackles behind the birds in the iron screen at the edge of the dining room. My father loves to light fires, and he keeps a fire going until almost summer. Under the table Marcus Garvey snorts and scrabbles for scraps, then falls into a deep sleep where he twitches and howls in some dream of hunting.

"That's nice, dear," my mother says. "Was it something simple?"

"Not particularly, a drawing of San Francisco; it's a story about an architect out there." My mother hands me the Canton serving dish of green vegetables dripping with Hollandaise. "I said no."

"Any particular reason?" My father sounds irritated; can he have cared about the publicity? His face is ruddy and angry-looking and he's drinking straight whiskey.

"She wanted to be a gentleman about it," Andrew says.

"I don't know—this sauce is wonderful, Mummy—I just didn't feel like it somehow. It was *my* drawing," I defend myself against my father's unspoken accusation.

"And what may I ask is the delicious dessert?" he asks, as if I hadn't been speaking to him.

"Caramel custard, dear."

"Andrew's in love again," I tease in a singsong voice, just the way I did when we were warring siblings coerced to the dinner table from our private redoubts—my bedroom with its rosy walls and college banners and all the other trappings of normalcy I could gather, and Andrew's dark cave, with its soccer posters and pornographic photography magazines hidden under the mattress.

"I *am* not"—he turns to Mummy—"Elizabeth's just jealous." At the dinner table we often have parallel conversations, where each child talks to the parent who is their provisional ally. My mother would support Andrew no matter who he was in love with.

"That's what they all say at first, the men who are in love with her," I say.

"So who is this siren, this irresistible exemplar of feminine temptation, this delectable *femme fatale*?" my father asks.

"Julie," I say.

"Ah, Julie, that turbulent creature," my father says dreamily.

"Watch out, she's a man-eater," my mother says. She will protect her precious little boy from the wiles of women.

"A witch, a man-eater; you women certainly do stick together," Andrew says. "How nice to be part of the sisterhood, to know that you can count on loyalty from your friends."

"A man-eater, but what a glorious meal," my father muses, off in his own world now. He has always admired Julie's style, the scent of roses which trails after her.

"She's a killer," my mother says.

"Mummy, she's a friend of mine, please," I say.

"I don't care, that's what I think," my mother says. "What can you see in a shallow woman like that, Drew?"

"What can he see in her?" my father rambles. "Men lured to death on the rocks, men turned into snorting, snuffling swine, the siren song and the twinkling lights that compel us onward. 'Tis not too late to seek a newer world!" My mother was always the practical one.

"I don't see anything in her." Andrew is defensive now, our jokes have gone too far. "She's an interesting lady, I'm going to help her with some legal problems. Anyway, if I *was* going to fall in love again, I *ought* to get involved with someone like that, according to Elizabeth. It would be a nice change to be the victim."

"So because of your guilt you're getting involved with a woman who is pathological about men, who hates men?" My mother's voice rises.

"The face that launched a thousand ships and burnt the topless towers of Ilium . . ." There's an edge to my father's voice now, as he takes a bite of the custard with his heavy shell-and-thread dessert spoon. He's making fun of his own erudition.

During our family dinner table conversations, my father often seems slightly apart from the rest of us as he sits there and carves the roast or dishes out the dessert. There's an intangible distance between my father and the rest of the world. It reminds me of the distance between him and the subject he's painting when he's working on a portrait. He stands at one side of the studio in front of the big easel. The subject of the portrait stands or sits posed on the other side, ten feet away, as the image slowly materializes a few inches from my father's heart. Even when he paints landscapes, the space between his brush and the scene in front of him—the ocean off the coast of Maine or an English rose garden in Connecticut—seems somehow acknowledged by nature, like an invisible atmospheric wall.

"For God's sake, you all," Andrew says, "I'm an adult! Don't you think I know anything about these things? Don't you think I can take care of myself?"

An adult who had a nervous breakdown, I think. An adult who takes a lot of lithium every day in order to function. "He's right," I say, not because I agree, but because I know that nothing will sink and turn the arrow more surely in his heart than Mummy's opposition and Daddy's fuzzy collusion.

"Look what she did to her poor husband," my mother presses on, "after the way he stood by her when she had that skiing accident, the way he took care of her!"

"Mummy, stop," I say.

We have talked about everything at this dinner table, with a fire in the grate and Marcus or his predecessors nudging our feet. We have talked about my adulterous affair with Sebastian, and Andrew's problems with Karen, and about my father's propensity for sleeping with young students and models. We have probably said things we shouldn't have; we've been through so much together. My father was often very poor, and sometimes very rich. Our parents alternated between redis-covered romantic love and bitter arguments punctuated with threats of divorce. In this volatile atmosphere, Andrew and I certainly never got the idea that there was anything wrong with any of this behavior. It was like feeding Marcus scraps from the table: harmless indulgence. We had our fun and other people could take care of themselves. If they couldn't, that was their problem. The only sin in our household was the failure to amuse.

"Let's go back to talking about my cover drawing," I say. "Maybe I can explain why I didn't want my name on it."

My father pushes his empty brandy snifter away and stands up from the table. My mother stands with him. Dinner is over. Through the big windows I see darkness covering the lawn and the trees and the flower beds that slope toward the swimming pool. There are pale-pink buds on the quince hedge, and a white tiara crowns the star magnolia across the brook. The days are longer now. Sebastian's with his children tonight, but tomorrow he's driving up for dinner with my family. Of course he knows them already, but I'm eager to have him here, to show him off to my parents and Andrew in his new context. We'll drive back to the city together Mon-day morning.

14

"Well, don't you like him?" I'm talking to Andrew, who's crouched in bed, reluctantly awakened by my shaking.

"Mmmmm, sure, very nice, very nice."

"Andrew, it's after ten o'clock!" Dinner with my parents and Sebastian and Andrew had gone well, I thought. There had been some silences, but my father had politely asked Sebastian a lot of questions about art dealing. Sebastian had answered with the accepted clichés and platitudes. With another person there, my family always behaved well. There was no gossip and none of that progression from criticism to sarcasm to incredulity that sometimes filled the boring moments at the family dinner table. "Liz," my father would say, "your table manners are terrible tonight." "Elizabeth," my mother would chime in, "don't you think it would be a nice idea to leave some muffins for the rest of us." "Is it *possible*," my father would finish off, "that no one ever taught you how to behave properly at a civilized dinner table?"

"Why should I get up, why don't you and Lover Boy go take a swim," Andrew says.

"He's reading the papers, a sacred time, silence must prevail," I say. "Come on, I'll make you coffee."

"Is Daddy down there?" Andrew groans and stretches. I can see that I've succeeded in convincing him to get up. "What's that?" An odd sound outside the window catches our attention. I hear a man's voice say something in a wheedling tone. "Nice doggie," it says, "bring it here." It's Sebastian. Andrew puts his finger to his lips and quietly gets out of bed to join me crouching at the window. Directly beneath us, two figures face each other across the sweep of gravel driveway. One is Sebastian, wearing his madder silk bathrobe, blue oxford pajama bottoms, and a single dark brown Italian loafer. The second figure is Marcus Garvey, lying on the gravel wagging his thick black tail. In his mouth is the other loafer.

"Come here, that's a good girl," Sebastian says in a voice I've never heard before. Marcus's tail wags faster, but he holds his ground. I can see that the thin, supple leather of the loafer is covered with drool. Sebastian takes a tentative hop step onto the driveway. "That's a good girl," he croons, "just give it here now." Andrew makes short explosive noises as he struggles not to laugh out loud. Marcus seems pleased at Sebastian's entreaties in spite of the mistake in gender. He stands up and wags his tail faster, but then he takes two steps backward, evening the distance between him and Sebastian. I slap Andrew reprovingly on the shoulder, but I'm giggling, too. Something keeps me from opening the window and rescuing Sebastian, although I know I should. I want to see what's going to happen.

"Oh, God." Andrew sucks in air, his face is red from the effort of holding in his hilarity. Sebastian tests his bare foot on the gravel and then draws it back again. Too sharp. He takes another hop step in Marcus's direction; his hair is uncombed and stands up away from his head.

"Give it here now, that's a good fella," Sebastian says. He's closing in on Marcus, who's standing about ten feet away, but just as he comes within grabbing distance, Marcus takes another few steps backward; the shoe dangles from his mouth. "Shit," Sebastian says, taking a few more quick hop steps. Andrew's hand is digging into my shoulder. *"Drop it!"* Sebastian shouts suddenly, in a much louder voice, and makes a lunge for the shoe. Marcus calmly sidesteps and Sebastian barely saves himself from sprawling painfully on the gravel. He scrambles back upright in a rage. "Goddamn son of a *bitch!*" he yells at the top of his lungs. "Drop it. *Drop!*" Marcus wags his tail in the friendliest way possible. After a moment he turns and trots down the driveway a few yards. Then he turns to face Sebastian, settles himself comfortably on the ground with a sigh of resignation at the silliness of humans, and begins a serious gnawing on the toe of the shoe.

"GIVE ME THAT SHOE!" Sebastian shouts. It's too late to rescue him now. Marcus stops chewing for a second and looks quizzically up at Sebastian. A window opens somewhere else in the house. "Nice doggie." Sebastian resumes his earlier wheedling tone. "Good girl."

"Good morning." Daddy appears in the doorway behind Sebastian. He's dressed in a crisp Brooks shirt and pressed chinos. "Something wrong?"

"I can't get the dog to give my shoe back," Sebastian says. His voice cracks with rage. His face looks contorted and flushed. His expensive bathrobe has fallen open.

"Marcus." My father's voice is crisp and commanding. "Give back the shoe." He walks over to the dog and takes the loafer out of his mouth, holding it carefully by the heel. "I don't think he's damaged it much," he says, handing it to Sebastian. "You know, dogs will be dogs."

"Thank you." Sebastian's control reasserts itself. "I guess I just didn't know how to ask him."

"Have you had breakfast?" My father opens the front door again and Sebastian follows him inside.

Andrew is now stretched out on the floor laughing. "I don't believe it," he's saying. "Oh, God, I don't believe it."

"I don't think it's that funny," I say.

"No, you weren't laughing! Not much!" Andrew's sitting up now, but he's still grinning obnoxiously.

"I'm going downstairs," I say. I'm angry at Andrew for witnessing my disloyalty. Downstairs, I find Sebastian in a new pair of shoes. His chewed loafer and its mate lie abandoned on the kitchen counter.

"What happened?" I ask. I pray my voice doesn't betray my secret.

"Your dog, my shoe" is all Sebastian says. He's reading the paper again. I pick up the chewed shoe and carefully wipe it off with a paper towel.

"It'll be okay," I say. "He does that, I should have warned

you." Sebastian doesn't answer. I reach into the kitchen cupboard for a rag and shoe polish, and cream the dented toe with Meltonian neutral. With the brush I buff it to a soft shine, trying to exorcise my guilt. "There, I'm taking them upstairs so he doesn't get hold of them again. Do you want to go back to the city before lunch?"

"Up to you," Sebastian says without looking up. I'm bothering him.

"Thanks for being so nice to my family," I say later, in the car.

"I've always liked your father," Sebastian says, once more his impeccable, assured self at the wheel of his car. "I never realized how much he drank." We drive through the spring air so sweet it permeates even the noxious fumes of the Connecticut Turnpike. In bed, I really try to thank him, undressing him when he says he has to leave and kissing his neck and face, laying him back on the bed and sucking him while I run my nails up and down his thighs, and then pulling him over on top of me, because that's what he likes best. But my secret lies between us. I've seen Sebastian come apart; I can't get it out of my mind. I remember Richard from the office once describing the open marriage he has with his wife. He explained that they both sleep with other people, but that they always tell each other. "It's not the infidelity that destroys a marriage," he said. "It's the secret."

"Don't go," I murmur at about midnight, when Sebastian's running water in the bathroom wakes me up.

"I'll call you in the morning," he says. "I have to get uptown." I stand next to him, me naked, him perfectly dressed, and reach up to kiss him. "Okay, if you have to," I say. "I can't wait until we can spend all our nights together."

"Mmm." Sebastian picks up his suitcase.

"I love you," I say, at the door.

"I love you," he says. I stand there and watch him walk down the stairs and wait until I hear the car starting up and pulling away from the curb. Then I go back to bed.

15 "I want to marry Sebastian and quit my job," I say, leaning forward in the leather chair, conscious of my body under a tight T-shirt and jeans. It's a hot day.

"Why didn't you want your name on the drawing?" Dr. Rosen asks. He fingers his flowered tie and creaks back in his chair.

"It's not my name, it's my father's name. I can't wait to be Smith, good old ordinary Smith."

"And you feel *that* will be your name?"

"It will be my married name."

"And that's the name you'll go under?"

"Sure. Sebastian's not the kind of guy who expects women to keep their maiden names. I'd have to put his name on anything I did, anything I signed."

"You're thinking of doing more drawings?" Now Dr. Rosen leans back toward his small, laboring air conditioner. Its noise blocks out the end of his question.

"A couple of people I knew in college are working as illustrators, they can go into advertising and make a fortune! But I don't know, I guess Sebastian will support me, too . . ."

"Have you talked about that?" Dr. Rosen's eyelids are drooping, maybe it's the heat.

"No, but he's an old-fashioned type; I mean I just know . . . He wanted Melissa to live through him, he said that's part of the problem, he's changed, but no one changes that much. It's hot in here."

"Is that the kind of marriage you want?"

"Who knows." I shrug my shoulders, this is boring. "That's the kind of marriage I would have, isn't it?" The chair itches

against my back; when I shift, my shirt sticks to the leather
because of the heat. Dr. Rosen swivels toward me in his chair
and stretches out his feet. His desk is piled with disorderly
stacks of letters and papers.

"You're so independent in some things, why are you willing
to turn this over to him?" he asks. I wonder if Dr. Rosen's
wife nags him about being so messy. I wonder if he's having
an affair, an affair with a woman who tells him that messiness
indicates largeness of spirit, an affair with a patient who's even
messier than he is. I glance over at the digital clock, our time
is almost up.

"Are you having an affair?" I ask.

"What made you think of that?" Dr. Rosen's eyes are wide
open now.

"Your desk," I say. "I don't know. Everything's going well,
but sometimes I feel like shit." The last few minutes of our
hour are the only time I tell the truth.

"You seem very depressed."

"But why should I be depressed? Sebastian's left his wife,
he's even moving out of the Stanhope. I'm doing okay at work.
My family's fine and I'm getting along with them. There's no
reason for me to be depressed." I remember that last night I
hadn't been able to sleep, that I had been up listening at the
door again, prowling because I thought I heard noises in the
hallway.

"People can have feelings without having reasons," Dr. Rosen says.

At work the phone messages from yesterday afternoon and
the hour this morning while I was at Dr. Rosen's look pre-
dictable. My mother—I've already talked with her. Ann Larsen
from Charivari—probably wants to complain about the ad
layouts. Andrew—I've already made a plan to have lunch with
him today at Da Silvano. The last pink slip brings me up short
like a push. *Patrick Casey*, it says in the receptionist's scrawl.
There's a San Francisco area code and number. What the
fuck does he want? I haven't spoken to him in two years, at

least two years. I take a deep breath and push the pink slips aside, but I can't help remembering a flash of Casey's wide-open laugh, his Irish face. Whatever he wants, he can eat his heart out. I have something good and certain now, I have Sebastian, I have security. I'm not going to chat with some old lover who never gave me anything but trouble. I have to ask you this, the doctor said: Are you sure?

I never thought I'd be in love with anyone again after I lost Pat Casey.

I'm late for lunch with Andrew, and I take a cab, which gets stuck in traffic on West Broadway near Gray Anderson's gallery. The driver, whose name on the license, Mohammed Kouvitsky, is almost obscured by grease stains, swears in some disjointed language at every other driver. The back seat sags, the ashtrays on the doors are overflowing with gum papers, and the cab stinks of the synthetic air purifier released from a red bottle on the dashboard. When I finally push through the glass doors, into the dim light and thick, garlicky smells of Da Silvano, I see that Andrew hasn't minded waiting for me—he's not alone. He and Julie have taken over one of the big tables next to the window, and an open bottle of champagne is cooling in a silver bucket next to his chair.

"Elizabeth!" He hails me as I refocus in the indoor light. He looks wonderful, his hair is disheveled and his white lawyer's shirt open. Julie is wearing a pale yellow silk shirt with big shoulders, and Andrew's yellow power necktie is looped around her neck.

"My darling," she says in her husky voice. I smell roses as she leans over to kiss me. "I thought we'd surprise you."

"I dropped in on Julie to pick up some papers on the way down and when she heard I was meeting *you* . . . I couldn't get rid of her." Andrew grins maniacally, his face is glowing and he lifts her hand to his lips in a courtly kiss. They smell of wine and intimacy, two gorgeous young animals ablaze with love and sex.

"Can I order?" I hurry the waiter when he comes to ask

what I want to drink. "It took me forever to get here, I'm late getting back already," I explain to Andrew.

"Don't be so uptight." He waves his arms expansively; his white shirtsleeves are rolled up, his watch flashes on the tanned curve of his forearm. "The afternoon is young. I thought we'd go for a walk, get high, swim in Bethesda Fountain. It's spring!"

"Some of us have work to do, I waste enough time with Sebastian." I sound prissy and disapproving. I hope that invoking Sebastian's name will make me feel less left out.

"Ahhh Sebastian, the man who loves dogs. Julie . . ." Andrew is laughing now, about to recount Sebastian's encounter with Marcus.

"Andrew!" I silence him.

"Ooooh, family secrets . . ." Andrew puts a finger to his lips and looks toward Julie; their eyes meet and hold for one long, flaming moment. They lean together, holding hands under the table.

"Now, Elizabeth always told me that little Andrew was the difficult child," Julie says. "He's not at all! He's an absolute pussycat, I don't know how anyone could think such a thing," and she turns and looks at Andrew as if he were the first man she had ever seen, the only man in the world.

"You've tamed me," he moans. The waiter brings my salad and I pick at it and spread the rest around on the big blue-and-white plate. My stomach is knotted in an acute attack of emotional claustrophobia.

"Look what he gave me last night, that bad wild crazy brother of yours who's supposed to be such a cad!" Julie holds out her delicate fingers to display a simple antique gold ring set with a luminescent opal.

"It's beautiful," I say. "Well done, Andrew."

"He says he plans to possess me completely," Julie whispers; then she throws back her head and lets out a peal of bell-like laughter that makes heads turn. She sounds like a delighted child. "He says the opal's inner fire reminds him of me!" She laughs again. She's making fun of him, and he loves it! He reaches out to lift the glossy curls off her fragile neck and breathe in that voluptuous rose perfume. I wonder if they took a few of Julie's little helpers before lunch.

"Inner fire," Andrew repeats in the besotted voice of an idiot.

"Are you going back uptown, or have you decided to give it all up for love?" I ask, trying to pass off sarcasm as humor and not succeeding.

"Give it all up for love," Andrew gurgles, leaning over to kiss the shoulder of Julie's shirt. He seems reduced to repeating the last phrase of anything either of us says.

"Don't be cross, angel." Julie strokes my arm and pouts her enchanting pout. At least she isn't too much in love to notice my discomfort. On the other hand, since it's Andrew and I don't want him to get hurt like all the others, I wish she *were* too much in love to notice. "He's wonderful, how could I not fall in love with him?" She sounds serious and I'm slightly mollified.

"Andrew, you do have to go back to work you bad boy, but not quite yet," she says to him. "First we'll have something yummy to keep body and soul together."

"Body and soul," Andrew murmurs in the direction of her neck. He straightens up slightly to order pasta, then leans back toward Julie as if she exerts a magnetic physical force. They hardly seem to notice when I kiss them both goodbye and leave, walking out into the relentless brightness of the sun on Sixth Avenue.

Even my desk at work feels like a safe haven after the turbulent air of lunch with my brother and my best friend. I dial Sebastian's number before I've sat down. I'll tell him about lunch and we'll laugh together at Andrew's fanaticism and Julie's fatal attraction. Gabrielle, the gallery assistant, says he's not there and she doesn't know when he'll be back. I think she's lying. His room at the Stanhope doesn't answer. No use calling Julie or Andrew; I get Ingrid's machine and hang up. The message from Casey is next to my phone, and without thinking about it I dial, but by the time I've heard the pings and scratches that precede a long-distance connection and he answers, my heart is throbbing and I can hardly breathe.

"Well, hello, Elizabeth!" His deep voice presses against my lungs like a hand. "Are you at work, same number?" he asks. "Can I call you right back?" I croak an assent and hang up. A drop of sweat slides down my side under my shirt. With Casey, "right back" could mean ten minutes, or it could mean three days. "Call me," he would say, but then he wouldn't be there. I'd call the local bar and leave a message, and the magazine he wrote for sometimes. Then I'd start calling the list of Casey's hangouts, political clubs, bars, restaurants. When I finally reached him he was usually busy interviewing someone or talking to someone else on another phone and he had to call me back. A lot of loving Casey had been waiting for Casey. I think I fell in love with Sebastian because he was always on time. I had waited for Casey to finish conversations, and waited for him to listen to other people's stories, and waited for him to put magazines to bed, and waited for him to finish articles—always waiting for him to put me first before his burning need to save the world or right its wrongs, or at least draw attention to them. Casey thrived on chaos; his apartment was littered with pink Final Notice slips and mailgrams from collection agencies. He never had time to open his mail. How could I have raised a child with a man like that?

After ten minutes of waiting for Casey I decide to call someone else so that my line will be busy if he does call. The hell with him and his seductive voice that brings back the pain. I dial the number Ingrid has given me for Ed Lissner.

"Mr. Lissner's wire"—a snooty English voice. I hadn't thought he was the secretary type.

"Elizabeth, thanks for calling me." Ed Lissner sounds thrilled. He doesn't put me on hold or ask if he can call me back.

"I don't really have anything to say," I say. "I just wanted to hear a sane voice."

"Life is somewhat hectic right now?"

"Well, my brother has fallen in love with my best friend; he's on lithium and she's an alcoholic who reduces men to gibbering idiots. I'm in trouble at work, and I just called an old lover and he put me on hold." As I pour out this litany, it begins to sound funny.

"Sounds interesting." Ed Lissner is laughing.

"It will be if I survive it." I'm breathing again.

"It's in the great artistic tradition. What did John Berryman say? Any ordeal that doesn't kill an artist is good for him?"

"Yeah, but it killed him."

"You're young yet."

"I'm not an artist, so why should I have to suffer like one? Didn't we already have this conversation?"

"I didn't listen," Ed Lissner says.

"That's one of my problems. I did a cover sketch for the magazine and couldn't bear to put my name on it. The editor was not pleased."

"It must have been pretty good; your magazine has great covers."

"There's something I like about sketching, remember that Rauschenberg drawing where he took a de Kooning and erased it?"

"How come it's sketching when you do it and drawing when Rauschenberg and de Kooning do it?"

"Aaargh, can we stop this?"

"Whatever you say," Ed Lissner says.

The office has emptied out and the cleaning men are dumping the wastebaskets into a big bin. I'm shutting drawers and getting ready to leave when the phone rings.

"Well, how are you!" It's Casey, of course.

"Reveling in your usual punctuality," I say. "Calling me back the same day. It must be important!"

"Of course it's important if it's you," he says. "What's going on in your life? I hear you're linked up with some art-world big shot."

"I had to pass the time somehow."

"And do you find the world of contemporary art utterly fascinating?" Casey has caught my sardonic edge.

"It *is* interesting, all the money, the collectors are bizarre, the traveling. There are *great* parties." I hope he's jealous. His voice sounds so much the same that it's hard to believe everything that happened was long ago. I concentrate on making the art world sound desirable, compelling, glamorous.

"I might be writing something about it," he says.

"It's not exactly your metier." The teasing flow of conversation has calmed me, my heartbeat is back to normal. I sit back in my chair and try to enjoy talking with Pat Casey. Maybe we'll be great friends. "I imagine you writing about crooked landlords or corrupt cops; you know, the *real* things."

"I have a problem with it, though; all my leads are coming from the auction houses and they're not exactly impartial. I thought maybe you knew someone who could help me out."

"The auction houses are run by a bunch of bankers now, a bunch of chiselers."

"*They* say the dealers are even worse, that people don't want to sell through dealers anymore. They come to the auction houses because then at least they know what the painting sells for."

"That's bullshit. The dealers have to protect the artists, have you thought of that? A lot of them even pay stipends; they're the real backbone of the art world. When artists don't produce, the dealers lose money!"

"But when they *do* produce, what kind of commission do the dealers take? And when they resell? You could help me with a lot of this."

"You're wrong. I know these people; if they were cheating, I'd know." Casey doesn't want to talk to me at all. It's the same old thing, the story comes first. That's why he called me back. Stories were always more important than people for him.

"Could you ask some questions for me?"

"I don't think so." He wants me to grill my new friends for the sake of his reporting. "These people are my friends now," I say.

"Okay, you don't have to get all hoity-toity," he says. "And don't go thinking this is the only reason I called you either!" He could always read my mind.

"No problem, it's nice to talk again," I say, mentally and emotionally slamming the door on his fat Irish face. "Listen, I have to go, the office is closing; let me call you back when I get home and we'll talk." I can't wait to not call *him* back.

"Okay, babe." He sounds sad now. "Maybe we shouldn't discuss the art world if it gets you uptight. Please call me, okay?"

"I'll talk to you soon," I say. "Goodbye." I hang up gently, pick up the telephone, and slam it down on my desk. Talk to you soon; fat fucking chance.

16 The swoops of the Bay Bridge appear and the outcropping of Alcatraz and Coit Tower almost block them out as I measure detail and perspective on the sketch pad. I've decided to do a series of drawings of San Francisco—for myself. The houses around Coit Tower are as big as my hand, Angel Island is the size of a fingernail. The sound of my lead against the rough paper is hypnotizing; I barely hear the horns and sirens of Houston Street at the end of the block.

The best drawings are the ones I don't do by myself. First I plan the composition, then I plot forms and angles and pencil in the largest shapes. I start shading and lining and slowly bringing each shape into focus, and it's then, while I'm mindlessly swinging my pencil against the page, that a line or a shape will appear which takes my breath away. It's never anything I planned; it's always the finest thing, and it usually determines the way I use the rest of the space. When I'm in this conscious unconsciousness, a door opening or the telephone ringing makes me jump like a frightened child. What happens when I'm drawing is the best argument I know for the existence of God.

Tonight, though, my anger keeps me from getting there. I put the Coit Tower aside and start on the Marin headlands and the choppy currents of the potato patch, and boil with resentment. Two years later he calls to pick my brain! I draw the towers of the Golden Gate and imagine the scathing things I'll say to Casey if he ever calls again, if he ever—oh, delicious thought!—is dumb enough to call and ask why I never called him back. Casey, who used to come in from California with no suitcase and run from the subway station and call me from under the window. He always wore the same clothes anyway, jeans and a plaid shirt and a blue blazer if it was absolutely necessary. Casey didn't have any money. If he had, he would have given it away. How could he have taken care of me? of me and a child?

I met him at a party in some nob's Nob Hill apartment on a magazine junket to San Francisco. I was in the middle of a stultifying conversation about the avant-garde in a huge living room with postcard views of the Bay, when I saw him. He came into the room like a thundercloud, a big man in a rumpled linen jacket and a pink plaid shirt who held himself as if he expected the rest of the world to get out of the way. Everyone knew who he was, but he walked right over to where I stood waiting for him. He lived in a tiny, ramshackle house at the back of Telegraph Hill, and that night he cooked dinner for me in his kitchen—a buttery omelette, wine, a salad, chocolate sauce so thick it turned hard when it hit the vanilla ice cream, more wine. While he cooked I played with his bulldog, Henry Luce, admired the views, and wondered why I was so ready to go to bed with someone I had just met. Falling in love with him was like being hit by a thunderbolt. I never understood it, and he never tried to.

"It happens," he would say. "Now it's happened to us." Then he'd go back to typing or talking on the telephone or reading the papers.

The Golden Gate begins to bore me, and I tear off another sheet and lay it on the floor. Using a book of aerial photographs that Casey gave me, I begin drawing the abstract shapes of the hills framed against the Bay in the background. The lines take on a surreal quality that seems promising. In New York it was different. There were dinners at Elaine's, where Casey gathered a group of fellow writers and politicians for hours of argument, conversation, and Jack Daniel's. A lot of his friends were famous, but he didn't seem to notice that. When the bar closed at 4 a.m. we'd go downtown and make furious, amazing love. Next to him I slept the sweet, dreamless sleep of contentment.

But I hated it when Casey was away. He could love me without seeing me. It was hard for me. I began to wonder about the future. My anxiety was rising when a slip of my diaphragm brought me face to face with it. The day I found out I was pregnant I couldn't even find Casey, he was down on the Mexican border interviewing illegal aliens. When I finally got him on the phone my voice was breaking.

"I'm pregnant," I said; then I burst into tears, of relief that he was on the other end of the line at last, of loneliness that he wasn't with me.

"That's terrific!" he said. "Congratulations!"

"It's a disaster," I sobbed.

"Come on, now we can get married. I've been thinking we should get married anyway. That's great! I've always wanted a kid."

"But how will we arrange it? Where will we live? What will we do?"

"Those are *details*! Those things don't matter, we'll work it out," he said, but his voice was so far away. Having a child was scary. Having a child with someone who might not be organized enough to help raise it, someone who didn't have any money and didn't want any, that was too overwhelming. An abortion was no big deal. Almost everyone I knew had had one. Karen had had two, Julie had had two, even Ingrid had had one. Later when we had worked things out, Casey and I could have a child. Only there wasn't any later.

When I talk to Dr. Rosen about Casey's call, he rocks forward, squeaking the springs in his chair.

"Why did it make you so angry?" he asks. He has a new air conditioner with an even louder roar.

"It reminded me of not coming first," I say.

"Other things are important to him."

"Too important," I say.

"What do you think would have happened if you had . . . if you had gone ahead with it? If the relationship had continued?" Dr. Rosen asks.

"I don't know. Sometimes I think he would have moved me out there, or moved to New York, and it would have been fine, better than fine, it would have been what should have happened. Other times . . . I don't know, I had to protect myself."

"It was never resolved," Dr. Rosen says.

"That's the trouble," I say.

"Did you decide together?"

"No, no, he was all for it. With him it's always full speed ahead. I decided. I talked to Julie. It was too much for me. I guess it was after that that I first came here." I remember recognizing that I needed help. The first shrink I went to kept hugging and kissing me and feeding me from his well-stocked refrigerator. The next one had a minimalist office with track lighting. Finding Dr. Rosen had felt like coming home. He was nice-looking and sympathetic, and best of all he said he didn't have time for me. I said I'd wait until he did.

"It bothered you," he says.

"Someone had to decide." I'm irritated at him now. "It's not one of those things where you can just wait around until everything becomes clear!"

"No, it's not," Dr. Rosen conceded.

"We all have to make compromises," I say, "every life is a bargain with fate. Mine isn't any different."

17 I ring the doorbell in the wall outside Sebastian's new loft and hear the scuffle and thump of children's footsteps. Bolts turn and click, the door slams open, and Alexandra Smith jumps frantically up and down in welcome, tight braids bobbing. Behind her stands Natasha, her dark-haired older sister.

"Kiss me first, kiss me first, please," Alexandra pipes in a little-girl falsetto. I've met the girls twice, when they were introduced with all the gravity of children's deportment lessons. They played at a picturesque distance on the Ninety-sixth Street swings while Sebastian and I trysted on a bench. As I lean down to kiss Alexandra, Natasha hurls herself at me with the force of a human missile.

"Sasha always gets everything first!" she howls. "I'm the oldest, you should kiss *me* first." She wraps her arms around my neck, twisting it down, and grabs at one of her sister's braids. Sasha collapses on the floor.

"Natty hurt me!" she wails. "Daddy, she *hurt* me!"

Natasha lets go and looks down in satisfaction. My vertebrae realign themselves. "Sissy," she hisses. "Elizabeth likes *me* better." Alexandra's crying escalates to a hiccupping sound. "Daa . . . aa . . . addy," she sobs from the floor. Her braids jerk compulsively and a small scabbed knee pokes from the hem of her flowered dress. I lean over to stroke her head.

"No!" her shriek echos off the walls. "I want Daddy!" Natasha looks on with disdain. "Oh, brother," she says.

"Daaaddy," Sasha coos inconsolably, cradling herself in the delicate angles of her arms. Sebastian, who has been standing paralyzed near the kitchen, snaps out of his trance and kneels next to her.

"It's all right, sweetie," he says. "Please, please stop crying." He pats her back tenderly while Natasha glares down at them.

"Leave her alone for a minute," I say. "Let her calm down."

"I'm here with you," Sebastian murmurs to Alexandra, ignoring me. "I'm going to take care of you." Her body is shaken by diminishing spasms. From the floor she looks up at me from her father's arms.

"It's dinnertime," Natasha announces. "We want hot dogs and microwave popcorn and ice cream for dessert."

"That's fine, but I don't have any popcorn, honey," Sebastian says from the floor. At this Sasha begins to sob again.

"We want pop-corn. We want pop-corn," Natasha chants, and her sister looks up and joins her. "We want POP-CORN," the two voices yowl in unison. "We want pop-corn."

"I'll go out and buy popcorn while Elizabeth fixes your hot dogs, and we do have chocolate ice cream, how about that!" Sebastian says.

"No! I want *you* to cook my hot dogs, not *her*." Natasha points an accusing finger at me.

"I'll tell you what—" Sebastian pretends to deliberate; in fact he has no choice. "We'll all go out and buy popcorn, and then we'll all come back and I'll cook dinner, okay?"

"And we can get some cookies and Fruit Roll-Ups and Froot Loops for breakfast, too," Sasha says, making a miraculous recovery.

"Are you allowed to eat that junk?" I ask.

Natasha looks at me with contempt. Should she even bother? I'm hardly a player anymore. I've been benched and her father has been run off the field. Her pale face squints as she considers.

"My mother says we can do anything we want here. She says Daddy should give us whatever we want."

It's almost an hour later when Sebastian returns, carrying Sasha, who is too tired to walk, and a bulging brown bag containing three coloring books, two plastic dolls in gold lamé with punk hairdos, two pink plastic ponies with matching pajamas, skating outfits for the ponies, a large rock, two jars of popcorn, a bag of caramels, and a giant box of cocoa and marshmallow cereal.

"We found an open toy store," he says, grinning crazily. I stare at him and boil water. There's nothing to say. I unpack the bag and open the garbage lid to toss out the rock.

"Stop!" A scream from Sasha. "That's my pet turtle, Daddy caught it for me. Daddy, she was going to kill Pokey!!" She pounds my legs and grabs the rock, cuddling it against her so that street dirt smears the flowered dress. It's another hour before they've eaten dinner, heard five bedtime stories, collected a hundred kisses, and settled provisionally into the new trundle bed. It's after ten by the time Sebastian stumbles back into the front room.

"I need a drink." He walks into the kitchen and comes back with a glass of dark whiskey, no ice.

"Rough night," I say.

"They're very upset, it's so hard for them."

"It's hard for you, too, having them act that way."

"At least they're showing their feelings. I'd be more worried if they were suppressing them. I'd be upset if they behaved well at this point."

"I wouldn't," I say.

"What's with you?"

"Don't you think they're manipulating you? Do you think it's a good idea to let them push us around like that?"

"I think I should make it as easy as I can for them."

"I don't think letting them behave badly is the same as making it easy! Pop-corn, pop-corn, we want pop-corn," I chant in a high, mocking voice. "That isn't any way to act and they know it. They're asking for limits. They're testing you!"

Sebastian is quiet, and as he sips the glass of bourbon his face takes on a stony expression I've never seen before. "I'm sorry that you don't like my children," he says.

"It's not that! They're terrific kids, I'm sure. It's just that they aren't behaving. Melissa wouldn't put up with that stuff."

"Melissa's their mother."

"That doesn't mean they have a right to drive us crazy!"

"You were pretty cold to them. They could sense that you didn't want them here. You didn't come out with us, you didn't help with dinner. You just sat in here and read a book."

"They didn't want me, they hate me! They want to have you to themselves."

"Elizabeth, they're little girls, they're babies, and they're in a frightening and confusing situation, a situation created by us. You're not competing with them."

"Of course you're right, I'm sorry." I smile and resolve to be different. I got what I wanted; this is the price. I will be a great stepmother, the exception to the rule about stepmothers. Then I remember that an exception to the rule just proves that the rule was wrong in the first place. "I'd like to spend some time alone with them," I say. "Maybe I'll take them up to the park tomorrow, we could go to the zoo." In truth, the prospect of spending time alone with the hysterical Sasha and the sullen Natasha makes me want to flee. They're not my children! They're not my problem! My feelings of anger and encroachment are intransigent. I decide to suppress them. I will make the children love me anyway.

"That would be great," Sebastian says. "Maybe I could get some work done. I promised I'd take them out for dinner tomorrow, and when I take them home on Sunday, I'm staying for dinner there so I can put them to bed—the psychiatrist thinks that will ease the transition."

"Both nights?"

"Then I've got crazy days Monday and Tuesday and dinners; the Mallet lawyers are driving me nuts. What a week."

"When are we going to see each other? I thought Monday was our day."

"They're suing me for the way I've managed the estate after everything I've done for them, a couple of spoiled brats!"

"Listen," I say, "after next week why don't we take a weekend off, go climbing or something?"

"Weekend?" Sebastian finally responds to me. "Weekends are when I have the girls."

"Okay, well, let's take a few days off during the week. The magazine owes me time, we can go to the beach or something, have some time alone."

"I can't do it. I'm way behind at work, there are a dozen artists whose work I promised I'd look at, and another show to install. I'm going crazy as it is; all this has taken a lot of time."

"We need time *together*."

"We're having time together right now. We're practically living together. My children are in strange beds, their mother is alone, we're together."

"I know it's hard, but we need some time to get our perspective back, to get a sense of humor about all this."

"I can't *afford* a few days off. Melissa's taking me to the cleaners, and I'm at a disadvantage because I moved out. Thank God, I sold the Nolan you didn't like. Listen, you wanted this, she didn't."

"What I wanted was you, to build a life with you."

At this Sebastian puts his head in his hands. It's all too much for him. I'm about to ask if *he* didn't want it, too, when I hear the patter of little feet approaching from behind him in the dark.

"Sasha's awake!" Natasha heralds her sister's appearance. "She woke me up!" In a moment Sasha is snuggling in her father's arms.

"What is it, honey?" He kisses her forehead and pushes her sleep-tousled hair off her face. "What's the trouble?"

"I can't sleep, it's strange here," she lisps in her adorable voice.

"Come on." Sebastian picks her up. "I'll put you back to bed and read you another story."

"And you'll soft my head?"

"I'll soft your head," he murmurs. His slender form, staggering under the weight of his smallest burden, is framed against the doorway for a moment and then disappears. "Of course I'll stay with you until you go to sleep." His voice carries out to where I'm sitting. "Of course I love you better than anyone else in the whole wide world."

18 "Elizabeth?" It's Julie's voice, with the thump of a piano and voices singing off-key in the background. Groping for the phone in the dark, I thought it might be Casey calling me the way he used to when he was working late and he missed me. Casey was no respecter of sleep.

"What time is it?"

"Don't be angry, angel. I don't know, it's about four." It sounds like Elaine's after closing time—the time when she locks the outside door and a few of the faithful stay on drinking and talking, and finally stumble out onto Second Avenue at dawn, jostling freshly wakened yuppies on their way downtown.

"Should I be?"

"Andrew and I just had the worst fight; he left here in a rage and I'm worried. I guess it's over with us." She gives a melodramatic sigh.

"Why are you worried?" I wonder if Andrew has been forgetting to take his lithium in the heat of passion, or if he has been mixing it with other things available from Julie's personal pharmacopia.

"He was just so angry! We'd had a lot to drink, I guess, and he said he was going to drive up to New Haven. He said he couldn't go back to his apartment because it would remind him of me, he'd go nuts there." Julie announces this disconcerting news in her breathy voice. Andrew is a scary driver at the best of times. "I guess we just don't have enough in common." She giggles at her own cliché.

"That can be an asset, for God's sake, it doesn't mean you have to drive each other crazy." I'm wide-awake now. If Julie's going to seduce my brother the way she seduces everyone else, at least she can have the courtesy not to casually dump him the way she dumps everyone else. "Sometimes, if someone has a lot in common, that's a problem, too—claustrophobia's a problem. You'd better get some sleep," I say.

"I'm too upset to sleep." The last word is slurred and I hear the noise of the telephone receiver dangling against the wall as Julie drops it for one of her sudden naps. She can nap anywhere, especially late at night. The sounds of the bar come closer through the receiver and I think about Casey, Casey at Elaine's, the bum. Casey, who didn't like to go outdoors except to stroll over to the newsstand and then down to the local Irish bar, where he would read the out-of-town papers and the tabloids and drink drafts, hunched over in his own familiar world, smelling the sawdust on the floor and hearing the drip of the beer tap and the litany of Irish jokes, and putting his bills down on the cigarette-burned plank.

"Who is it?" Julie's nap is over.

"I'm worried about Andrew," I say. What's the point of being angry at Julie? It's like being angry at the rain.

"Come on up here and have a drink."

"You should go home. I'll call my mother and see if he got there. Don't worry. It's not your fault." If Andrew is in an accident on the turnpike, whose fault will it be?

"Okay, angel, talk tomorrow. Kiss, kiss." I look across at the clock; if Andrew is driving to New Haven, he won't be there yet. I want to call Sebastian, to talk to someone, but I know he would hate that. Sebastian is a great respecter of sleep. I lie back down and stare out at the streetlights and leafy trees. When I wake up again at eight, I call my parents.

"Andrew's in bed," my mother says. "He's sleeping late. Is it important?"

"I was worried about him. He had a fight with Julie."

"Oh, *her*," my mother says. "He's fine."

"Did he say anything to you?" I'm always looking for my mother's agreement, for acknowledgment of my feelings. Was *I* crazy to worry about Andrew?

"She was never good for him," my mother says. "She hates men, it just took him awhile to realize that." Her voice is smug and certain.

"Okay," I say. "Tell him I called."

I'm still punchy nine hours later as I walk with Ingrid through the rooms of Sebastian's gallery, which is hung with Jake Gander's latest work—ragged swatches of canvas glued onto shaped frames and painted with layers of Day-Glo paint, which protrudes from the picture plane in weird, sexual shapes. Ingrid stops to assess each one, moving back and forth in front of it as if the canvas is a prism which gives back the light at different angles as she moves.

Through the wall I hear Sebastian crooning in the low, seductive voice he uses for important clients. At the edge of the doorway to his office I see Amelia Polker, former stewardess and show girl, and now the socially prominent wife of George Polker III of Cleveland, Ohio, and East Hampton, New York. Ever since G.P. III jettisoned his boring Shaker Heights wife two years ago and married the supple-legged Amelia, they have been amassing an "important" collection of contemporary art. This involves spending the vast inheritance George has from his father's discovery of a laxative formula, allowing themselves to be shamelessly courted by museum presidents and trustees who long to put them on the board and lay claim to their burgeoning collection, and buying paintings from Sebastian at astronomical prices. They listen to Sebastian because the paintings for which they pay these ridiculous sums are soon worth even more ridiculous sums. That's G.P. III's idea of good artistic judgment.

Recently, G.P. III has decided to build a private museum, an architect-designed addition to their house, which looks like Tara. Sebastian detests private museums. He says collectors who build them have a King Tut complex. They violate the first principle of all great collectors—that important work should eventually be made available to the public. Many of the artists in Polker's collection have sold him their paintings with the understanding that they would someday be in a major museum. Now they won't be. But the Polkers' buying and selling is a gold mine of commissions for any dealer they do business with. I know they've just given Sebastian a black Stella to sell. So of course he doesn't say anything to them about what he thinks of private museums.

"It sounds very exciting," I hear him oozing as a sliver of G.P. III's English suit appears at the edge of the doorway. "Won't that be Mark Darling's first private commission?" The Polkers have hired the architect of the moment—famous for the Adelphi Insurance Towers in Duluth and an addition to the San José Museum of Art.

"We're quite excited," Polker says in the Harvard accent he has nurtured since the cradle. His skin is rich and leathery, like the hide of the bears and hippos rich boys have in their rooms at college.

"He's not cheap!" In spite of voice lessons and Italian lessons, Amelia still slips occasionally into a New York quack. Her husband gives her a modulating look. Julie has told me that Amelia Polker was once famous for the things she did with her tongue.

"Nothing good is inexpensive these days," Sebastian says comfortingly, putting a hand on her sleeve as if they could all remember the fine old days of Wasp ascendancy, when some things were for a special few, regardless of money. "What a lovely dress," he adds, nodding at her blue linen sailor suit in a way which is admiring but carefully asexual.

"It ought to be," la belle Amelia quacks. "I had to go to Paris three times to get it right!"

"You don't think we're asking too much for the Stella?" G.P. III interrupts. "Half a mil," he mutters almost to himself. Sebastian smiles reassuringly. "Don't worry, I'll see what I can do," he says. The Polkers have crossed the room and stand near us next to the elevator doors. Deftly, just as the elevator arrives, Sebastian turns and brings the four of us together. This way the Polkers will have the thrill of meeting Ingrid, the understanding that important young artists hang around the gallery, but there won't be time for conversation.

"Oh yes," G.P. III says when he hears Ingrid's name. I'm impressed and pissed off. Sebastian, who has left his wife for me, is behaving as if I were just another pretty visitor, a pleasant appendage of Ingrid's. He's sucking up to fools; but he's sucking up brilliantly! The sunlit gallery space filled with the sold paintings, the murmur of his secretaries and assistants contracting international business, the confirmation of Mark Darling's excellence sought and given, are all evidence of Sebastian's power. It's all very well for artists to complain about the crassness of collectors. They *are* crass. But it's these crass collectors who make the art world turn. It's their unspeakably vulgar money, made on oil-well widgets and supermarket chains, that enables artists like my father and Jake Gander and Ingrid and the rest of them to go on painting. I can't wait to marry Sebastian and have dinner at the Polkers'. I want to go to their famous Paul Rudolph–designed town house, nicknamed The Kelvinator for its utilitarian ugliness, and eat veal and morels at their famously boring dinner parties.

As the elevator door shuts, Sebastian switches off his unctuous gentleman manner and turns to us. A pretty secretary rushes out from the inner office. "Jake Gander's on the phone, he's furious about the *Times* review, and the Mallets' lawyer."

"Tell them to hold," he says. "Where are you two lovelies going now?" He gives me a proprietary kiss on the cheek.

"How much can you get for an early Stella these days?" Ingrid asks.

"We're going over to Brooklyn to see the Robert Wilson," I say. "Ingrid has tickets, but . . ." I wish Sebastian would come with us. I know he has two calls on hold and a million things to do.

"Polker wants at least five hundred," he says to Ingrid. "The Robert Wilson, that sounds interesting. So you won't be home until late." Robert Wilson's shortest works are *long*. I'm beginning to regret going. Does Sebastian mean that if I came home earlier we could see each other? I haven't moved into the loft. He says it would complicate his separation negotiations.

"What's your commission on a deal like that?" Ingrid asks.

"Second-market deals are usually a twenty percent commission, but I may not get their price. No deal, no commission."

"Or you might get more," Ingrid says.

"I'll call you later," Sebastian says to me. "I have an ADAA dinner." Sebastian is leading a campaign against the auction houses supported by the Art Dealers Association of America.

"Okay." I'm not happy, but he doesn't notice. He gives me another perfunctory kiss and turns to hurry back toward the inner rooms, with their ringing telephones and bright young assistants and shelves of art books and catalogues. It's hard to get a man's attention; I wonder just what it was that Amelia did with her tongue.

19

"It's lucky I left plenty of time," Ingrid says. She has hired a car to take us to Brooklyn, but we're stopped dead in traffic at the entrance to the Brooklyn Bridge.

"I guess we'd better get used to sitting." I think of the patience and concentration that Wilson's theatrical genius requires of his audience.

"I wonder what Sebastian will get for that Stella," Ingrid says. Nothing interests artists more than other artists' prices.

"He's a brilliant salesman," I say. "You saw the way he snowed the Polkers. He can sell anything!"

"That's why he's a dealer. I can't believe this traffic."

"He had a lousy little Paddy Nolan last year, and he even got a good price for that!"

"That must have been the one the Kresses sold, to some Japanese industrialist. I heard they weren't asking for much, they knew it wasn't a good painting."

"Sebastian was pleased," I say. "Do you think we'd do better on the Manhattan Bridge?"

"It's just rush-hour traffic, there's no avoiding it. I hope we'll move faster once we're on the bridge. Do you know how much commission Sebastian gets on Gander's work?"

"Fifty, I suppose. Isn't that the usual?"

"Most of them don't go by the usual, most of them take as much commission as they can get. Someone told me that Jack Griese won't even *take* a picture to sell unless he knows he can make a hundred percent profit. See, we're moving now."

"Then how much does the seller get?"

"That's the point, the seller gets eighty percent of what they asked for—they get what they expect to get."

"And the dealer gets the rest?" We're moving off the other end of the bridge now and turning down toward Flatbush Avenue, past the delis and drugstores of Brooklyn Heights and past the Watchtower building, where a crowd of Jehovah's Witnesses wait outside for the pamphlets they will distribute to homecoming commuters. "What's to keep the seller from finding out? I mean, can't the Kresses just ask Sebastian who bought the painting and how much they paid?"

"Of course not, the dealers can't give away their secrets. If the Kresses knew who wanted a Nolan, why would they need Sebastian? They'd just go directly to the buyer. A lot of these buyers want to keep it secret anyway; they have tax problems, things like that. I often don't know who buys my work when it's resold. It's all hush-hush and that's the dealer's advantage."

"You can't expect them to put themselves out of business!" I'm bored with Ingrid's arguments against dealers and against collectors and against everyone except painters in general and herself in particular.

"They're all riding on our backs; if it weren't for the painters, they wouldn't have anything to sell."

"I guess everyone thinks that *they're* the indispensable link," I say.

"Yes, but the painters really are."

We sit in the small, darkened theater and watch as a golden light suffuses the stage. High above us in the uppermost tier of boxes a man dressed as Garibaldi sings a Philip Glass piece to an Indian on stage. Later, a black pole bisects the space. As slowly increased light allows us to focus, the pole fattens to become the figure of Abraham Lincoln, his top hat and beard defying gravity as he hovers horizontally above the footlights. I relax in my seat and remember other Robert Wilson performances. Lucinda Childs's jerky task movements and the huge train in *Einstein on the Beach,* and the cat legs which looked as if a giant feline was walking behind the curtain from left to right in *The King of Spain.* I will myself into the dazed suspension of intelligence in which long performance pieces become enjoyable.

It's almost midnight when Ingrid's car drops me at the corner of Sullivan Street, and I walk quickly toward my doorway, staying close to the curb. The criminal is an opportunist. I try to look as if I'm meeting a large male companion. At my steps I carefully check the street and surrounding buildings before taking out my keys. The lights in Julie's house are blazing, probably someone new taking in her act; the little dinner in the garden, the casual attitude toward her own exquisite pos-sessions, the tossed hair and the smell of roses on a summer night. I contemplate interrupting her, but what if it's Andrew, back from New Haven for a reconciliation. Besides, I don't want to miss Sebastian's call.

"How was the Robert Wilson?" he asks. The call wakes me from a drowsy sleep; it's my second bad night and I look over and see that it's after six o'clock in the morning.

"Intense," I say. Sebastian laughs, but there's something wrong with his laugh. Then there's silence.

"What's wrong?" I sit up in bed, still wearing the black slacks and sweater I collapsed in when I came home. They smell of limousine and the Brooklyn Academy of Music.

"Everything," Sebastian says. I know right away what's wrong.

"Like what?"

"Elizabeth." A ragged sigh comes through the receiver. "It's just too hard for me."

"Where are you?"

"At home, in the study; the children are still asleep. What an awful night!"

"What an awful day," I say.

"You have every right to be angry with me." His voice is stilted now, as if he has rehearsed this. "But I hope you'll let me explain."

"There's nothing to explain, is there?"

"I guess not." Now he sounds defeated.

"You made a decision, and now you've chickened out," I say. He doesn't answer. I feel nauseated, but I know there won't be any relief in vomiting; it's a kind of erosive nausea I remember from other griefs, other partings. We're locked in our own miseries.

"Elizabeth," he says finally. It sounds as if he's crying. "Are you still there?"

"Yes, although I don't know why."

"It's the little girls," he says. "It's nothing to do with Melissa. I just can't go on hurting my children like this."

"You think this won't hurt them? First their father moves into the Stanhope, then he sets up housekeeping with some bimbo, then he comes home like a whipped dog? Do you think it's good for them to live with parents who hate each other?" But I have told Sebastian all this before, many times. When he's with me, he believes me. When he's with Melissa, he believes her, and as he swings wildly back and forth, we're all jerked and pulled along like the tail of a kite.

"You're not a bimbo! Oh, Elizabeth, if you knew how confused I am!"

"That's pretty obvious."

"I just don't feel that I can tear my family apart right now because of what I want. It's too abrupt, it's too merciless."

"Are you saying that you'll be able to do it in the future? How many times are you planning to change your mind? That's the worst thing you can do to all of us! You were certainly ready to leave last week—you *had* left."

"Elizabeth, I don't know what to do. I can't think straight anymore." I begin to cry as it all sinks in. Sebastian has gone back to Melissa, he will always go back to Melissa.

"Oh, God, don't cry. I have to see you," he says.

"Fuck you," I say, crying.

"When can I see you today?" My collapse seems to have strengthened him.

"Get lost! You've made your choice."

"Please, Elizabeth, this is as painful for me as it is for you."

"Bullshit! Don't tell me about the pain you're in because of my pain. You're *causing* my pain, there's a big difference! What am I supposed to tell you—that it's fine, that I understand perfectly, I'm supposed to comfort you? Jesus, Sebastian! I love you, what did you expect?"

"I love you, too," he says. I'm silent, numb.

"I want to see you right now," he says. "Please, I have to see you."

"Good luck. Melissa won't even let you out."

"Fuck her."

"Oh, you probably already have, haven't you? You've probably already consummated the renaissance of your perfect marriage with some perfect sex, right?"

"You are so outrageous!" Sebastian sounds completely recovered. "Do you think I could really do that, after you?"

"I think you're capable of anything."

"I'll be down there at noon; if you don't want to see me don't be there, but I'm coming."

"Okay," I say.

"Okay, you'll be there?"

"Maybe." But I have given in and he knows it. Through the blinds I see trees in leaf and the tops of the buildings across the way with their frieze of fruits and garlands. To the right is a long lintel decorated with astrological signs, a crab, a lion, a ram, and a unicorn. I wonder what long-ago Italian builder decided that a unicorn belonged in a horoscope. I roll off the bed, still in my black clothes, and head for the kitchen and coffee. The apartment traps me; I'm already wondering if Sebastian will call again. To get away from the phone I brush my hair, stuff ten dollars in my pocket, and head uptown for a coffee shop.

Outside Julie's house I hesitate. She usually has an early coffee at Tosca, the corner restaurant where the Italian owner flirts with her and spikes her espresso with Calvados. I could ring the bell, but instead I walk uptown toward NYU and the student places that open early. Inside the door of one I pick up the *Daily News*: SENATE VOTES BILL PROTECTING AGED AND DISABLED FROM MAJOR ILLNESS. Idly I notice that that's impossible. The booths are filled with fresh-faced students chatting or reading notes. At the counter a few stools are empty. On one a big man reads a glossy art magazine. It takes me a minute to recognize Ed Lissner.

20 "We can't go on meeting this way," I say, sitting next to Ed Lissner and hoping the joke will distract him from my tear-streaked face and slept-in clothes.

"Hey, Elizabeth." He hails me in his flat, loud voice. "What are you doing here?"

"Feeling old," I say. "These students look embryonic." The waiter brings me coffee and a muffin I didn't order. Maybe Ed has a regular morning companion who has a muffin and coffee.

"Too young," he says. "Their minds are undifferentiated, unformed, uninteresting."

"Ahhh, but their bodies!" I sip the coffee, it's rich and strong. "You teach them," I say.

"As I get older, I'm increasingly bored; it's a real problem. Even their bodies begin to look boring. The same questions, the same answers, the same propositions."

"But look at the other end of the spectrum, the *overdifferentiated* mind," I say, nodding at the article Ed Lissner is reading in *Artforum* by Martin Marx, a critic famous for his convoluted ideas expressed in impenetrable prose.

"I'd hate to hear you on the rest of the art establishment!" Ed Lissner laughs.

"You know it as well as I do. Novelty passes for art; confidence is mistaken for genius. Real art should change your life. Real art should be talent informed by vision! Otherwise what good is it except to hang on the walls of rich people's overdecorated apartments?"

"That's a big order." Ed Lissner's interest is a cool compress on my raw nerves. The muffin tastes fruity and sweet—an hour ago I thought I'd never eat again. "Well, isn't that what happens when you look at the Turners at the Frick or the Monets at the Met? Those paintings change your perception. They blow the top of your head off—that's what Thomas Higginson said poetry should do, and he was right."

"No wonder you don't want to try to be an artist," Ed Lissner says.

"Oh, not this again." I bite into the muffin and hit a plump, sweet constellation of raisins.

"No, not now at least," he says. "I have to go and counsel some of those embryonic minds. Stay and finish, maybe we can have lunch someday."

I finish the muffin before despair breaks through the restorative haze of Ed Lissner's admiration. Where is Sebastian right now? Dressing for work, bantering with Melissa, chatting gaily about their future together. I swallow the last of the coffee, it tastes like turpentine. From the phone booth I call Julie, and before she has a chance to say anything I don't want to hear, I surprise us both by bursting into tears. "I'm sorry," I weep into the receiver. "I can't help it." The pain is back in force, as if during the hour it left me alone it was only gathering strength. "He's gone back to her," I say between sobs.

"Are you sure?" Julie sounds rational and wide-awake.

"He says he loves me but he can't bear to leave the children. He wants to see me, but how can he stay with her if he loves me so much?" I go back to crying, but the trough of my feelings is not as deep.

"Are you going to see him?"

"He's coming to my apartment at noon."

"Elizabeth, don't see him, refuse to see him. I think you should force a decision right now."

"How can I?"

"He's dishonest and he's dragging you down with him. The weak can destroy the strong."

"Maybe I'm weak."

"I don't think so, it's the situation that's weakening you. You have to take a stand."

"But if he sees me and we make love . . . I *love* him!" This seems truer than ever, as if I didn't understand the force of my love until it was spelled out in pain.

"You've loved other people, too; you've never lived with Sebastian. You fell in love with him a long time ago—you were very vulnerable." I hear her moving around the kitchen, the clink of ice cubes against a glass, the first one of the day.

"I'm vulnerable now."

"Not the way you were after Casey."

"Do you have to bring him up?" I'm crying again. "He *really* fucked me over." Casey deserted me and now Sebastian has deserted me.

"And this is a walk in the park?"

"Is your love life so perfect? Shit, Julie, I need support from you, not criticism."

"I'm sorry, it just makes me furious the way Sebastian's jerking you around. I don't think he's ever going to come through. He may marry you, but he'll never pull his own weight. You're always going to be forgiving him and nursing him along the way you are now. You deserve something better!"

"I *like* nursing him along." The phone beeps and an operator interrupts us. I fish in my pocket and deposit another quarter.

"I don't think you always will," Julie is saying. "You needed someone like that. He's not a match for you."

"You sound so calculating."

"Women can't afford to be sentimental."

"But I want him!" Sebastian appears in a shimmering haze of desirability. His importance in the outside world, his famous gallery, his glittering social life, his perfect body are all unattainable. "I have to see him," I say.

"And he can't resist you. Oh well, I'll love you whatever you do. Meet me at the corner for coffee, okay? It's only ten-thirty."

At home I peel off my rumpled clothes, take a long shower, and put on a fresh shirt and jeans, which flatten my stomach like a girdle. As I step into the street I notice just for a moment that it's a perfect spring day, cool and promising, with sunlight filtering through the pale of new green leaves and borders of red tulips in the iron enclosures around the plane trees. As I turn right onto Bleecker, there's a whiff of sweet hyacinth from the back gardens. But under everything is pain, the hard handful of stones resting at the bottom of my stomach, the obsessive replaying of Sebastian's conversation. I blame myself completely, without imagining for a moment that my behavior is not the cause of everyone else's actions. Julie is at a table against the wall, her spiked coffee half gone, wearing a long denim skirt with batik patches and a soft leather jacket.

"Angel!" She blows a kiss across the table, then winces as if her arm had cramped. Her pale face is luminous in the dim light. "Tony, another coffee just like this one," she calls to the waiter. "You need it," she says to me. I sit in the straight wooden chair across from her. The sunlight streaming through the open door is a long way off.

"The first of May," she says. "Isn't this the perfect first of May?"

"I don't want to talk about the weather."

"Still cranky?"

"You don't know what it's like. You've never been dumped."

"You're not being dumped. You're being given a warning which you choose to ignore."

"Do you have to be so down on him!" The Calvados burns warmth into my throat and unravels the knots in my guts.

"Sorry. I'm in a shitty mood this morning, these chairs are so damned uncomfortable." In the most matter-of-fact way possible, Julie takes a syringe and a tiny bottle out of her jacket pocket, plunges the syringe into the bottle, draws out the clear liquid, hikes up her long skirt, and plunges the needle into her thigh. The whole thing takes about ten seconds. The room is dark and empty and no one notices. She looks up at my startled face and grimaces.

"It's the only thing that helps," she says.

"What is it?"

"Something the doctor gave me."

"Dr. Wilson?"

"That old fogey! Are you kidding. He's so conservative he won't even prescribe vitamin shots. He wouldn't give me anything to help. No, it's Mike Gilman, a nice doctor I met a few weeks ago at one of Marcia Halsman's parties."

"You've been going out with a doctor?"

"I see him sometimes. It's not like Andrew." Julie gives me an assessing look. We haven't talked about this. "I was really in love with your brother," she says.

"And this doctor you're going out with gives you morphine?"

"Look, it's much easier than going to someone like Wilson: no making appointments, no waiting for hours in those musty waiting rooms reading old magazines, no snippy nurses."

"Does this guy have a license to practice? Is he really an M.D.?"

"Elizabeth, do you think they give this stuff out to laymen? Come on, don't be so shocked; my neck and upper back have been really bad. Mike thinks I have a pinched nerve from the skiing accident that was never properly treated. This is just another way of dealing with the medical establishment."

"He thinks this is the proper treatment, morphine for breakfast? Does he know how much you're drinking? Isn't that dangerous?"

"Would I do anything that *wasn't* dangerous?" Julie tosses her head and that contagious laughter fills the dark room. Tony smiles from the bar; it looks as if he's about to break into a chorus of "O Sole Mio." Julie raises her hand to order another. I hope Mike Gilman knows what he's doing, I hope he knows who he's dealing with. If he doesn't, I hope he loses his license. I hope he goes to jail.

When I walk back through the door to the staircase up to my apartment, Sebastian is sitting on the stairs. His face is drawn and pale, his eyes red.

"You look awful." I lean over to kiss him as if nothing were more natural than meeting him here, crouched at my door.

"You didn't want to see me, you hate me!" His voice cracks.

"Well, here I am. Come on, you look as if you need some coffee." The two cups of coffee and Calvados combined with Sebastian's physical presence cure me. There's nothing we can't work out.

"Oh, Elizabeth!" Upstairs he collapses on the couch, his head buried in his hands again. "I thought I'd never see you after this morning." His narrow shoulders in a blue polo shirt make him look like a little boy with a little boy's inconsolable sorrow. I sit next to him and put my arms around him, murmuring his name.

"I don't know what to do," he says. "I just don't know what to do."

"You don't have to decide anything right now. You've been up all night, you're wrecked. Just calm down."

"It's so hard," he says. "I feel as if all these things are spinning around in my brain, I feel so helpless."

"Of course you do," I say. "You're exhausted, you're under more pressure than anyone could bear."

"Melissa's so certain, it convinces me when I'm with her, I really don't know what I think anymore."

"Give yourself a little time," I say, stroking his back with one arm around him. "These *are* important decisions, don't let anyone pressure you."

"I'm so confused, I just seem to hurt everyone I care about!" Sebastian's head sinks lower. I stroke his back with both hands and lean into him.

"You've been up all night, of course you feel confused. Take it easy, wait until you feel better."

"I can't give you up," he says to the floor. "That's one thing I know. I can't give you up."

"There there, you don't have to," I say, slipping my arms around his waist and kissing the back of his neck. "You don't have to."

21 The Cushing Rehabilitation Unit of Mt. Sinai Hospital is in a Beaux Arts mansion on Ninety-third Street that was owned by Billy Rose in his heyday. A grand staircase leads from the marble, chandeliered entranceway to second-floor bedrooms where arched French doors look out onto the ruins of formal gardens. The bathroom off the big bedroom has mirrored walls engraved in a frieze of flowery erotica. Above the sink two bezeled satyrs chase a voluptuous nymph through a grove.

"He had to import glass cutters from Europe for this," Julie says. "The Americans were too prudish." In the next room six beds are lined up under the garlanded ceilings, and old chandelier fixtures are replaced with fluorescent tubing. A woman with thinning hair slumps on one of the cots.

"I hate it here." Julie lowers her voice to a hiss in the dim light. "There's no fucking privacy, they don't even let you use the telephone! I'll kill Mike Gilman when I get out!"

"Maybe he wanted to help you."

"By betraying me? By turning me in? I don't need his self-righteous help. How does he know I belong in here?"

"He must have known . . ."

"He tricked me into coming here. Stupid Bonita, just because she couldn't wake me up one morning she has to call Gilman! Couldn't she have called old Dr. Wilson for once? I was fine."

"I guess she didn't know . . ."

"Do *you* think I belong here?" Julie's fury tears through my platitudes. "It's a total mistake! There's a heroin addict in my room and an ex-prostitute the cops turned in; maybe I had some problems, but these people are crazy!"

"Of course, you're not like them."

"Fucking Gilman should spend some time in here himself before he sends someone else. They make you do these ridiculous jobs. I have to wait on tables and bag the garbage, it's disgusting! It's easy enough to hire people for that—it's not as if this place is cheap!"

"You haven't been here long, maybe it gets better, maybe it's some kind of initiation," I say. I don't know what to say. A nymph in torn gauze lies panting behind Julie, her sister is being rogered from behind by another satyr.

"It's not going to change, the people are shit! There's no one with any education or background at all! In my room there's the junkie and the whore, a woman whose husband kicked her out of the house in Chappaqua, and a Lenox Hill nurse with a Demerol habit. What am I ever going to have in common with them?"

"Nothing." It doesn't seem to matter what I say, anyway.

"There's all this God stuff, it's all emotional-crutch shit, the opium of the masses! We have to sit around in groups and discuss our feelings, and they're always crying! When you say your name, they chant hello like a bunch of Moonies! They're already on my back because I did so well with men. They're just jealous! Why do I flirt so much? my counselor keeps asking. Naturally they assigned me to some tough old dyke. A *man* would understand."

"What's wrong with flirting?" I ask. A young woman with black hair cut like a boy's appears in the doorway.

"You gonna be in there all day, princess?"

Julie doesn't answer. "Nurse Jane Fuzzyhead," she says in a whisper. "They say I've abused men, that I've abused my power over other people. Well, the men didn't seem to mind!" She laughs a sweet laugh of triumphant memory.

"They sure didn't," I say, but I remember Harvey West, and Andrew, my brother.

"You've always been my best friend," Julie says, putting a frail hand on my shoulder. "Listen, would you do me a favor?"

"Sure."

"When you leave, tell the guy at the desk that you're going to bring back my copy of the Bible, okay? Then go to my house. Bonita will let you in. In the library there's a red-leather-bound Bible that's really a safe. Dump out the jewelry in there and buy a pint of Calvados or brandy, anything, and drop it by for me. Will you do that?"

"Hey, princess!" The dark-haired girl is back again, sneering. "You think the crapper is your private quarters or something?" She has a strident New York accent.

"Fuck off, you little spic," Julie says, but she guides me out of the room into the bedroom and out to the hallway. "Would you do that for me?" she says, turning to face me again.

"I'll try," I say. "If I can find it." I'll have to tell her that Bonita wouldn't let me in.

"It's on the third shelf from the bottom in the middle on the east side, you can't miss it," she says.

Downstairs in the great ballroom where Diamond Horseshoe girls waltzed with railroad millionaires, Cushing patients and their visitors sip brackish coffee at round tables on folding chairs. It's easy to spot the patients, quiet men and women who are either being solicitous or repentant, or just fidgeting out the time until the painful visit is over. Julie and I wait in line for our coffee and handful of supermarket chocolate cookies.

"They want to bring my mother here, for a family session," Julie says when we're sitting. "Can you imagine what she'll make of all this? Her beautiful daughter in a sweat suit!" Her mother's possible discomfiture seems to amuse her. Julie's mother lives in Paris with the fourth-rate French count who is her fifth husband. Her father is dead, killed on an Italian racetrack near Rome when his car spun out of control a long time ago.

"Is she coming?" I ask. Julie shrugs as if the answer isn't important.

"Maybe she'll have to face what she did to me," she says. Julie rarely talks about her childhood. I have a vague impression of grand-hotel living, bluffing creditors, dressing up for parties, and lecherous stepfathers. "It might be interesting, actually. Can you imagine what this must have been like?" She looks around the room now, wide-eyed like a little girl. "Billy Rose and Fanny; remember *Funny Girl*, wasn't that a great movie! They lived exactly the way they wanted to live." I nod. The chatter of visitors is shattered by a blaring bell, and two burly men in brown uniforms appear in the doorway. They don't bother with the amenities at Cushing. Visiting hours are over. Julie gaily kisses the air on both sides of my cheeks, but as I kiss her back her mood downshifts to sadness.

"Come back and see me next week, please." She seems to be pleading with me and begging my pardon at the same time. I can't tell if she's also referring to the spiked Bible. "I never had anyone to talk to except you," and then she turns quickly back and lightly walks across the marble floors to the curved staircase with its polished brass risers and glittering past.

22

"Can I see this one?" I reach into the third bin, where the densely hatched corner of a Jasper Johns drawing has caught my eye.

"Whoa, Elizabeth!" Sebastian takes my hand off the picture, which he gently eases out into the room, leaning it against the wall. "I have high hopes for this one," he says.

"How did you do with the Polkers' Stella?" The crosshatching seems to draw me toward it; the intensity of the design is rich, deeper than black, like the inside of a stairwell.

"Not badly." Sebastian smiles a smug smile. "I had a buyer in Los Angeles who had been looking for one of those early black paintings."

"So they paid . . ."

"A million two." Sebastian finishes my sentence.

"I bet that made George Polker happy; he thought even half a million was too much to ask, remember? Will you do as well on the Johns?"

"Better." Sebastian hesitates, as if he's going to say something else, but then he tenderly replaces the Johns and pulls out two Bud Partin paintings. He's about to install a show of the young painter whose work is the explosion of the spring season.

"It's fantastic that you got Bud Partin, what a coup," I say.

"He couldn't resist the idea of Martin Marx writing the catalogue, and Martin owed me a favor." Once again, Sebastian seems on the verge of saying something else. He looks over at me questioningly.

"Remember when we fucked back here?" I say. "I was terrified that that Mallet was going to fall over on us!"

"We shouldn't have done that, it was crazy."

"It was fun," I say.

"Listen, I have piles of boring stuff to do back here before lunch. I'll meet you out front. Why don't you go out and charm whoever is out there, pretty girl."

Thrilled to be part of Sebastian's team, I wander out into Sebastian's gleaming public rooms. A few groups of people are milling around, looking at the show of ceramic tea sets by a California sculptor which are about to make way for the great Bud Partin. Standing alone in front of one of the tea sets is Sue Stanley, the dealer I met last winter at Ingrid's show.

"Hi. Elizabeth Cole, we met last winter," I say.

"Hello!" She apparently remembers me. "Aren't these exciting pieces," she invites my agreement. I'm about to tell her how much trouble Sebastian has had selling them when I remember that my job is to charm people. Sue Stanley is a California dealer and the tea-set genius is a California artist.

"They almost seem to float in this space," I say, sounding phony. "Sebastian's about to install a Bud Partin show!"

"Don't tell me you like *that* work!" Sue Stanley snaps. "One of the nice things about San Francisco is that my collectors aren't caught up in this frenzy for the superficial output of hyped-up hotshots with MFAs." Yes, I think to myself, they prefer paint-by-the-number seascapes or scenes from the Old West.

"What are you showing now?" I ask, privately deciding that Sue Stanley is terminally out of it.

"I'm trying to put together some illustration shows. San Francisco has such a great tradition of magazine and newspaper drawings, really because of the Hearst papers, Winsor McCay and Erté . . . I'm trying to get some contemporary equivalents and it's discouraging. No one can draw anymore!"

"Elizabeth can draw," a deep voice says. I turn and see that Ed Lissner has stepped out of the elevator and caught the tail end of our conversation. "In fact she did a glorious drawing for the cover of *Antics* this month." I cringe at Ed Lissner's boosterism and thank God he's not brandishing a copy of the magazine.

| 129

"We can all draw," I say. "Art has gone beyond that now."

"San Francisco!" Sue Stanley turns a glittering, acquisitive eye on me. "I don't suppose you have any more drawings in your studio?"

"I don't even really *have* a studio," I say.

"When could I drop by?" Sue Stanley asks.

"Ed, I'll kill you!" I say to the grinning culprit.

"For what?" Sebastian has materialized at my right shoulder.

"I was just saying I'd like to see Elizabeth's drawings," Sue Stanley says, introducing herself to Sebastian.

"And I was seconding the motion," Ed Lissner says. He sticks a square hand toward Sebastian. "Hello," he says, "Ed Lissner. Nice to meet you."

Sebastian steps back as if someone has pushed him. "Dr. Lissner! It's an honor to have you in the gallery."

"Oh, the honor is mine," Ed Lissner says, but he's still looking at me. "I was lured here by these lovely ladies." Then he reaches out and puts a hand on my shoulder, as if to keep me from moving off if his conversation with Sebastian gets boring.

"Would you allow me to show you around?" Sebastian's manner is subservient and courtly at the same time. It's not as unctuous as his rich collector's manner, but it's equally deferential. "I have a few interesting pictures in the back," he says. "I hope you won't mind my saying how much I liked your book on Jackson Pollock, it was extraordinary. I meant to write you. A rare combination of passion and scholarship."

"Oh, thank you." Ed Lissner is polite but distant, as if he's heard all this before. As he moves off with Sebastian for his obligatory look in the back bins, he turns and gives me a smile of pure, merry complicity.

"I wonder who suggested to Lissner that he drop by the gallery," Sebastian says later, at lunch. "He has a reputation for never looking at pictures after they're hung, he doesn't want to be influenced by the installation—a real purist."

"I think he came to meet Sue Stanley. I didn't realize he was such a big deal."

"They were both definitely impressed by the Partin work I showed them," Sebastian says. I stare down at my pumpkin ravioli in nutmeg sauce and long for spaghetti and meatballs. "He certainly seemed interested in *you*, Elizabeth." He stares accusingly across the tablecloth.

"Ed Lissner?" Something about Sebastian's interrogatory manner makes me feel guilty. "I suppose he is. He's never really made a pass, though. I met him at Ingrid's last winter, he's a friend of hers." I look up into Sebastian's angry face.

"And why didn't I hear about this new friendship?"

"I didn't think you'd be interested, we aren't living together. I meet a lot of people I don't mention to you."

"A lot of single, wealthy, successful men?"

I shrug. Who knew that Ed Lissner was wealthy? "A few, I guess. I was never that impressed with Ed Lissner, to tell the truth; he knows I'm involved with someone."

"Does he know it's me?"

"Sebastian, until recently you were very married; our affair was a secret, remember?"

"I don't mean to act like a jealous old man," Sebastian says. "It's just that you're so pretty and sparkly sometimes and I don't really have any claim on you."

"I love you. That's a claim."

"Anyway, I'm sorry to be so touchy. Ed Lissner obviously thinks a lot of you. It would be great if you'd put in a word about the Partin show."

"I will if you want, but I don't think it would make any difference. He's a man who knows his own mind."

"You seem to have a lot of respect for him!"

"I like him, he's been very kind to me. A couple of times this winter he really gave me a hand." I remember Ed Lissner's admiration on the morning of Sebastian's short-lived decision to go back to Melissa.

"They say he's gay." Sebastian searches my face for clues.

"I don't think so. People just say that about any man who isn't married."

"How do *you* know?"

"It's just a feeling I have, for God's sake; maybe he is gay, I don't know. I don't care either." I'm pleased by Sebastian's show of jealousy, but I protect my small friendship with Ed Lissner as if it was fragile and precious. If I subject it to Sebastian's envious scrutiny, it will lose its power to help me. "It's just a friendship," I say. "I'm a lot closer to Julie, even to Ingrid."

"But they're women."

"It's not what you're thinking, that's all I'm going to say. Come on, don't sulk; let's go back to your loft and I'll show you exactly what kind of friendship it isn't."

Sebastian laughs and his possessive fit seems to disperse. We order cappuccinos and talk about the Partin show and the latest feud at the Museum of Modern Art and the scandal over the Greek statue the Getty bought, which the Italians are saying was stolen from an archaeological dig in Morgantina. I don't mention Sue Stanley's interest in my drawings. It will probably come to nothing anyway. We leave high and laughing. Outside the restaurant on Prince Street bright flags are waving in front of the stores and the sun warms my skin through the silk shirt I wore for lunch with Sebastian. He leans over and presses me toward him, kissing me and turning me to look at my face.

"Let's get married," he says.

"What is it that you're afraid of?" Dr. Rosen asks. It's late afternoon now, the sun is fading, and Sebastian wants to marry me. I'm intolerably tense and jumpy, as if my nerves were raw wounds on the surface of my skin.

"I don't know." I hate Dr. Rosen for asking stupid questions. I hate the grind of the air conditioner and the horns from distant traffic. "Maybe I'm disappointed because if I marry him I can't marry you."

"Do you think I'm married?"

"I don't care! I just feel terrible. I'm exhausted, too much has happened."

"What about the prospect of showing your work. Is that making you uncomfortable?"

"My work isn't good enough, I'm not good enough. I suppose it's all right for some San Francisco tourist gallery, but that's a joke. It's not a real gallery!"

"What do you imagine?"

"I imagine myself alone, on some beach, away from all this. It's too much to sort out. I know, it's all good, I should be feeling happy and grateful, but I don't, I feel terrible!"

"It's important to listen to your feelings."

"Stop preaching!"

"Okay, let's backtrack. You say you're not good enough. What does that mean?"

"It's just the way I've always felt. I'm an impostor. If anyone knew what I was really like . . . it's that I'm not good enough to be an artist, to be a member of my family, not good enough to be a member of the human race."

"Are you afraid of what your family will think?"

"It's more complicated than that! My family's so unstable, so crazy, I never know what they'll think. If I marry Sebastian, my father might approve or he might be furious—I never know. I'm sick of being so *out there*. I want to lead a normal life. I want safety. Maybe Andrew wants that, too," I say. My mother has told me that Andrew's seeing Karen again. "I want to be safe, doesn't everyone want that?"

"And being an artist isn't safe?"

"It's safe for my father because he's a man. I know that women aren't supposed to be artists. They're supposed to be beautiful and marry rich men and have cute towheaded children. Imagine Ed Lissner being rich. That was a surprise."

"You could have done that."

"I'm *going* to do that. I'm going to marry Sebastian and be the perfect New York wife and have perfect kids. I know I'll have to convince him, we're older than the ideal, but it's close enough. It's the best I can do."

"Sometimes we have to live out our wishes to see how empty they are," Dr. Rosen says. There's a spot on the lapel of his seersucker suit.

"I guess so." What a platitude! I need a smarter shrink. Behind him the last light silhouettes the chimney pipes and fire escapes and the copper roof of a church steeple against the evening sky.

23 It's cooler, the last June day before the scorching, humid heat of the New York summer, when everyone who can afford to leaves the city, and the bongo drums from the park and the blare of ghetto blasters on the empty streets throb a crazy score to simmering insanity. The art world goes to Europe, for the International Art Fair in Basel and the Venice Biennale, and to Vence and St. Tropez, the rich people go to the Hamptons, and everyone else just gets the hell out. The pavements stink, lights and air conditioners flicker and stall as the city's power transformers overload and blow out, there are fires under the streets and old people stuck in elevators. The bums take over and the civil war whose DMZ is Ninety-sixth Street boils perilously fast and threatens all of the city's carefully defined and well-protected lives. Sebastian's in Santo Domingo getting a quickie divorce, Andrew and Karen are engaged again, and I'm on my way to visit Julie, who is a few days away from the end of her twenty-eight-day treatment at Cushing.

She meets me in the grand entry hall, looking like a college kid in a raincoat with rolled-up sleeves, jeans, and ballet slippers. When we leave the building she looks both ways up and down Ninety-third Street, as if she's a little frightened of the streets where she was once queen. I'm frightened myself. I'm afraid that she'll guide me right around the corner to a bar, where she'll order coffee and Calvados, or down to the Surrey Liquor Shop for that pint I never smuggled her, or that she'll march me into a drugstore to have an illegal prescription filled, or demand that I get her out of Cushing early. I take her arm, heading her firmly toward the park, and imagine myself squirming under some suspicious pharmacist's glare as I explain that my aging mother has a back condition which requires these extraordinary drugs, or sitting in Dr. Gilman's office getting nowhere as I try to explain why Julie doesn't belong in a rehab.

In the park, runners and bicyclists pass us on the road as we walk downtown under the arch of trees. The bridle path is white from falling pear blossoms and a few horsemen canter by in full fox-hunting regalia, sending the joggers and dog walkers off the path into the woods. A light rain begins to fall, it's almost as if there's an element of water in the air. I put up my red umbrella, which bathes Julie in a rosy aureole of light. Behind the Metropolitan Museum, near the great blank glass walls which house the Temple of Dendur, we sit on a bench.

"It's been a beautiful spring," I say, relaxing slightly. Fifteen minutes of our hour is up and she hasn't asked for anything yet. "Can you see the garden from your window?"

"I'm beginning to." Julie turns and leans against my shoulder with a sigh; instead of roses there's a light scent of soap and clean clothes. "I won't bite you, Elizabeth," she says. "You don't have to worry."

"You look great," I say. "You look terrific with no makeup."

"I was so pissed when they took it away! You should have heard me. I didn't really think that anyone could like me if I wasn't wearing eyeliner and mascara and some blusher. I was afraid I wouldn't even recognize myself. And my clothes! they wouldn't even let me wear my own clothes!"

"It sounds like prison," I say.

"It is in a way. What I learned is that even without the way I look it's still me. I've even stopped looking in mirrors, and I haven't weighed myself since I got there."

"But how you look *is* important. *You* taught me that! I remember you saying that you never left the house unless you looked great, because you never knew who you might meet."

"Did I really say that? But why would I want to impress someone who cared so much about how I looked?" Instead of answering that how you look creates first impressions or that how you look defines who you are—Julie's old answers—I watch as runners labor past, some sweating and grunting, others in an outer zone of physical endurance which makes them look as if they are traveling slightly above the asphalt.

"I never came up to this park," Julie says. "I used to hate to leave the Village."

"It's still dangerous," I say, remembering old headlines. "See those big trees behind the museum; that's where Jennifer Levin was killed."

"That could have happened to me, that could have happened so easily."

"Come on! You wouldn't go off like that with someone you hardly knew!"

"Late at night, stoned on something, I would have thought it was a great adventure. I was always going to bed with men I hardly knew! And men are so strong! When you're out of it you forget how strong they are."

"Not all men are like that, though!"

"Who knows what someone is going to be like under those conditions. I drove men crazy—I loved driving them crazy! It was my way of having fun. I thought I could tell, you know, which ones were dangerous and which were safe. I thought caution was for other people."

"But you *could* tell. You *didn't* get hurt."

"Blind luck." Julie stretches and breathes deeply, putting her hands behind her head. "Pure blind luck, or a benevolent God."

"You can't start worrying about things like that in this city. You'd get paralyzed."

"I'm not talking about worrying, I'm talking about having a teensy bit of good sense."

"I think you're being too hard on yourself," I say. This is always a safe remark in any situation.

"What's been happening with you, tell me about the outside world. How's your family, Sebastian, your job?" Julie gets up off the bench and I join her, heading north. Our conversation is oddly disjointed, as if we're people who've just met.

"Sebastian proposed," I say. "He's in Santo Domingo getting his divorce."

"You're kidding!" Julie grins and gives me a big hug. I stand uncomfortably in her arms, feeling her slender body through the raincoat and smelling the fresh smell of her hair. I don't think I've ever been hugged by a woman before. "That's great." She lets me go and stands back. "How are you feeling about it?"

"I'm not sure." Julie's interested eyes encourage me. Who else can I talk with? "I thought I'd be totally happy, you know it's just what I wanted. Instead, I don't feel much at all."

"You mean you're not as sure as when you didn't think you could have him?" We turn out of the park at Eighty-ninth Street and up past the big gray Church of the Heavenly Rest. There are curtains of wisteria blooming on the terrace of the Cooper-Hewitt.

"I guess that's it. I'm thinking a lot about Casey lately. Now that Sebastian's decided, he's busy all the time."

"You're going to marry Sebastian and you've been thinking about Patrick Casey?"

"I guess it's probably natural. When you make a decision, you think about all the things you give up—all those other possibilities. It's just that with Casey I was always so certain. At least that's the way I remember it. Of course, everything else was wrong about it; he didn't have any money and he was so irresponsible, or responsible to other things. Maybe I was just younger."

Julie has never liked Sebastian and I expect her to make much of my nostalgia. Not that she was so crazy about Casey either. "Give yourself some time if you need it," she says instead. "You've waited a long time for Sebastian, he can wait awhile for you. You don't have to decide today."

"But I have decided!" I miss Julie's opinionated advice. In the old days she would have told me not to be ridiculous, marrying Sebastian was the best thing I could do, or else she would have said I *had* to at least sleep with Casey again before I did anything. As we approach the broad steps outside Cushing, another woman waves from the street.

"Yo, princess!" she shouts. She's walking next to an older woman in a black dress. For a moment I think she's insulting Julie, but they embrace each other and I realize that it's Dolores, Julie's dark-haired roommate, who had been waiting to use the bathroom when I visited. "Fuck off, you little spic," Julie had said.

"Dolores, this is my friend Elizabeth." She steps back but keeps an arm around Dolores.

"This is my mother." Dolores introduces us in an accent that sounds as if she's chewing gum, although she's not. Dolores's mother and I look blankly at each other as Julie and Dolores chatter and hold hands, kiss us goodbye, and trip up the steps like two schoolgirls after vacation.

"It's a wonderful place," Dolores's mother says in her broken English as we stand together in their wake.

"It's a wonderful place," I echo, but I wonder. Why does everything have to change?

24 Everyone has doubts, don't they? There are hundreds of stories about girls who are so frightened that they have to be pushed up the aisle by their bridesmaids, and men getting drunk with their best men and finally being practically poured into the church. It's the natural thing. So when Sebastian and I drive up to New Haven and wait in line and fill out the forms I don't say anything. He's preoccupied anyway. The Partin show got lukewarm reviews and Partin is threatening to find a new gallery. His daughters are increasingly upset and demanding, demands orchestrated by the vengeful Melissa, and he's planning a big George Mallet exhibit for the last show of the season before the art world takes off for Europe. I know Sebastian will be going too, at least to Paris and probably to Basel, but we haven't talked about our summer plans at all; there's barely time to talk about our wedding plans.

Julie takes me to Bloomingdale's and Saks, and we end up buying a sexy white silk suit at a boutique near Jaap Reitman's bookstore in SoHo. Even with a small wedding there are big conflicts. My mother doesn't like the silk suit, and when she finds out that Julie helped me buy it, she grimaces and says nothing. How could I have known that she wanted to go shopping with me for the dress, the way mothers traditionally do? She never went shopping with me before in her life!

Andrew tells me that I have to invite Karen. Since I've told Julie that *she* can't come because of Andrew, I don't see why I should. Andrew says he won't come without her. I tell him to do what he wants.

Sebastian has his own dramas. He doesn't tell me that his little girls want to be flower girls; instead, he tries to explain to them—unsuccessfully—that there are no flower girls at a small wedding. Their mother tells them they aren't wanted. He promises to race to their house after the wedding with a piece of wedding cake and flowers for each of them.

Tension is high, any one of us could go off like a string of firecrackers. But the wedding itself is beautiful. We stand out on the lawn of my parents' house with balloons that Andrew and Karen brought tethered to the hydrangea bushes. Late-afternoon light slants across the velvety grass as Judge Harold Brinkley marries us in the brief, simple ceremony that has the most complex, long-term effects of any legal proceeding any-where. Afterward we all drink champagne and eat a white cake from the local bakery and set the balloons free and watch together as they float lazily up to the tops of the trees and beyond in the summer evening air. Then my father brings out a bottle of Napoleon cognac that he says he's always saved for my wedding and we all drink that, and for a while everything seems absolutely wonderful. Andrew and a kid from next door tie a can and a shoe to the back of the car and write *Just Married* on the back window with soap. By the time we leave, turning down the driveway and into our new life together, my father has gone upstairs to take a nap and my mother's in the kitchen cleaning up.

I snuggle next to Sebastian as he turns onto the turnpike from the New Haven ramp. I'm a married woman.

"When do you think I should move my stuff into the loft?" I ask.

"Don't you want to keep your apartment? It's such a good deal."

"I don't know. Maybe I could keep it as a studio, but it's kind of inconvenient. I thought I could get something closer, maybe even in the same building."

"It's an expensive building and it's all rental—money down the drain."

"Maybe we should buy something. I like it down there south of Houston."

"Elizabeth, I just moved!" Sebastian's voice goes up a few notes.

"Sorry." My voice rattles and I feel like crying.

"What's the matter?" he says impatiently. Huge trucks boom by us in the night.

"It's just that you sound so withdrawn. I mean, we just got married!"

"I can't believe this! You are always making trouble at the worst times, Elizabeth. You're like a child! Of course I'm preoccupied, I have a lot of things to take care of—you should be able to take care of yourself, at least. I've divorced Melissa and married you. I can't buy anything for us right now, I'm still carrying my old apartment as well as the gallery space, to say nothing of alimony and child support."

"I'm sorry," I say, feeling very sorry . . . for myself. "Maybe Daddy would lend us some money." I wish I had the kind of father who slips a big check to his beloved daughter on her wedding day, or even the kind who says he'd like to help out. My father had said nothing. He is too much off in his own world to think about practical things.

"I can't take money from your father."

"He'd be giving it to me, as a wedding present." We're on the Bruckner now, passing through the swampy flats and over the drawbridge south of Pelham; the lights of a huge barge slip along in the narrow channel to the right. At the edge of the road a burned-out car rests on rusted rims. "I don't see what's wrong with that."

"I didn't think you would." Sebastian slows the car to turn onto Willis Avenue and the ramp up to the bridge. Two black kids in torn shirts approach, wielding wet squeegees. Sebastian rolls up the window and the door locks clunk shut.

"Perhaps you could explain it." Now *I'm* being sarcastic.

"This is a difficult time for me, I thought you understood that." One of the kids yells as Sebastian guns the car into the turn and away.

"You wanted to get married, it wasn't my idea."

"Yes," Sebastian says. "I did."

"Are we going to spend the rest of our lives paying for what we've done? What if I want to have children?"

"Anything like that is out of the question!" Sebastian's voice squeaks with panic. "Can't you be a little patient!" He turns off the drive at Houston Street and heads west.

"I'm sorry," I say again. I think about what it would be like to be with another man, a Casey or an Ed Lissner. Someone who hasn't done all the things he wants to do already—or isn't frightened of doing them again.

"Here we are." Instead of putting the car in the garage, Sebastian has pulled up to the curb in front of the loft. He unlocks the doors and waits for me to get out.

"Where are you going?"

"I promised I'd drop in on the kids, I've got wedding cake for them, it's already late."

"Shit," I say, opening the door. "Some wedding night." Then I'm sorry I've said it.

"I love you, Elizabeth," Sebastian says. "This wouldn't make any sense if I didn't love you." I shut the door and hear the automatic locks reset as he drives off. Upstairs in the loft I pour a brandy and wonder who to call. I started with brandy, I'll stick with brandy. There are messages on Sebastian's service from his lawyer and from Sue Stanley. She was mildly enthusiastic about my drawings and said she wanted to include them in a group show. I know that if I call her tonight she'll say she's changed her mind. I sit on the leather sofa and try not to remember all the dreams I've had about a wedding night. The dreams began with Cinderella and Snow White and all the little girls who married princes, and they sustained me through the fierce loneliness of adolescence and the panic of being abandoned by a father who couldn't pay attention and a mother with an eye for an attractive carpenter. I try to keep from thinking about all the other wedding nights that everyone else in the world has had: ecstatic nights on shipboard, with the moon gleaming silver on the Gulf, nights in tropical hotels with ceiling fans and latticework like a Bogart movie, stormy nights on the North Atlantic coast cuddling under a down quilt while the winds rage and the shutters bang and waves crash and boom against the beach at the foot of the dunes. When I get up to refill my glass, I walk over to the phone and call Julie.

"Angel, how was it?" she says. "Where are you?" Instead of answering I burst into tears and pour out the whole story.

"That does sound a little rough. Her voice is warm and sympathetic and this makes me cry harder. "Do you want to come over here, do you want to meet me somewhere?"

"No." I sniffle. "I just want to go home."

"Then *go* home." Julie knows exactly what I mean by home. "Leave Sebastian a note. He can call you." For a moment she pauses as if there's something else she's thinking of saying but doesn't. "You sound as if you need some sleep," she says.

"I really can? Won't his feelings be hurt?" Her advice cuts through my mental haze with the force of a revelation.

"You're entitled to take care of yourself."

"That's what he said; he said I should take care of myself."

"It's a difficult time," Julie says.

"But it shouldn't be!"

" 'Shouldn't' is a stupid word. You feel what you feel, there's no point in saying that you shouldn't feel that way. You have your feelings and Sebastian has his."

"But I want them to match!"

"Which is worse? If they don't match, or if you turn into an emotional chameleon and take whatever form is convenient for him?"

"I thought you were through with giving advice."

Julie laughs. "It's a hard habit to break."

"I'm glad you haven't."

"Okay, here is my last advice. Make a cup of coffee, leave a really nice note for Sebastian telling him that you love him, and go home. You'll feel better. I'll call you in the morning."

"You're right," I say. "I will." So instead of waiting up for Sebastian, and drinking another glass of brandy, and insisting that we have it out right now, tonight, I wash my face, straighten my clothes, catch a cab on Prince, and walk up my familiar stairs in a glow of brandy and exhaustion. Something has changed, though. A part of me has detached from Sebastian and his problems and become my own. I spend my wedding night in my comfortable old bed curled up around the other pillow. In the morning I have a headache, and a husband.

25

"I want you to look great for this," Sebastian says. "It's an important night for me."

"My debut," I mumble. We're in bed, and out the big loft windows I can see that it's just dawn. For days before this opening, Sebastian has been getting up at six and going to bed after midnight.

"A lot of people would kill to come to this opening; we've been flooded with requests." Sebastian sounds pleased, but lately his voice and actions have seemed speeded up, as if he were a 33 rpm record being played at 78 rpms.

"Why is it so important?" I say. I keep drifting back into sleep; it's begun to feel like an act of disloyalty to get eight hours a night. "You own most of the paintings in this show anyway."

"But I don't want to own them forever, that's the point."

"You could sell them tomorrow, couldn't you?" The room is bathed in half-light; snatches of dream drift in and out of my consciousness.

"Not at the prices I want to get. I need this show and some great reviews of Mallet as a painter, and maybe even a hot auction to get them there. The Sotheby's contemporary auction helped, but not enough."

"Didn't it set all kinds of records?" I hope that Sebastian's answer will be long so that I can get back to sleep, lulled by the comforting sound of his voice. Lately it doesn't seem to matter to him if there's anyone listening. I think about his friendship with George Mallet, his good luck in being named executor of the estate. In my fractured dreams George Mallet is breaststroking across our swimming pool in New Haven. When I wake up, Sebastian is in the living room drinking coffee and making notes from catalogues and slides. I drift off again, and when I wake up he's on the phone, so it must be after nine o'clock by now. The last week has been a succession of disasters. The electricians messed up the lights at the gallery! The walls were painted the wrong color white! The invitations had to be redone. The Polkers were coming in on the Concorde from London and had to be met at the airport. My petty problems, my frictions with Judith Grimes-Gurewitz about sending my San Francisco drawings out for Sue Stanley's show, my fears when Sue said that she's scheduled it for the beginning of July, all seem minor compared to Sebastian's unending crises. He has a deadline! Whatever happens reflects on him! And there's a great deal of money at stake. Under pressure Sebastian retreats to a position of self-pity. He is the most beleaguered and unfortunate of men, dogged by incompetence, plagued by the necessity of dealing with idiot collectors and temperamental artists, weighed down by guilt about his children. I know that any pressure from me will reduce his view of me to just another person who wants something from him.

The day of the opening the heat breaks. The sky is a glorious June blue I notice in the moments that I spend being chaperoned by Julie from the hairdresser to the makeup lesson and then to the manicure place. As we finally dress for the big moment, Sebastian's face is set; he whispers to himself incessantly, going over a dozen internal checklists. As we leave, he finally turns to check me out. I'm a young woman transformed into a high-class ornament by a very expensive red silk dress with a matching jacket, a manicure and pedicure, and a Kenneth hairdo. I've been waxed, streaked, painted, massaged, cut, blown-dry, and exercised—all for love.

"Good." That's all he says, then it's into the elevator and the waiting car.

At the gallery we walk into an empty room. Gabrielle is waiting in an astonishing swath of pink chiffon, the other assistants chatter behind her, but within fifteen minutes we've been separated by the crowd, which seems to burst in waves from the big elevator into the waiting space. Lucy Pinbottom rushes up to congratulate me on being married to such a *handsome* man. Her husband, Donald, a froglike figure with real-estate holdings all over the world, lurks in the background. Caroline Bayer says how *fantabulous* I look, darling. Oliver Remsen comes over to say hello, but his attention is behind me on the elevator in case Julie arrives. Ingrid is there in a flowing blue caftan, and through the crowd I see Ed Lissner's big, comforting square head. He seems to be squiring a dark-haired woman young enough to be a student. She hangs on to him as if she might be lost in the swirling crowd if she let go. So he's not immune to those perfect bodies, after all. Occasionally I glimpse Sebastian, greeting guests, talking about the pictures, accepting congratulations on the installation. He looks absurdly handsome as he charms and sparkles for Jim Buckman from St. Louis and Anna Biddle, who has a small gallery in Philadelphia. In another corner Harry Nicolaitis, a Greek collector, is coming on to Gabrielle. I see Ernst Bayer in the mob around one of the bars, and Hilda Anderson, Gray's alcoholic wife, has trapped Bud Partin against the wall near the elevators. The noise level rises to the deep roar which signifies a successful party. The art has become incidental.

I drift in and out of conversation with the Pinbottoms, with the Polkers. I've just been intercepted by Odlie Bergin, a Swiss dealer who's opening a New York gallery, when Julie floats out of the elevator in a pale lavender dress. Since Cushing, her presence has become perceptibly lighter, as if she were carrying less weight.

"Elizabeth." She touches my shoulder. "You do look wonderful! It's amazing what an afternoon can do." In her face I can see that what I really look is different, and in the sireny red dress I feel that I've inherited the sensual heaviness of Julie's old persona.

"Am I ever glad to see you! My face hurts from smiling."

"It's a great success. Why don't you relax and enjoy it, take some credit."

"Credit for nursing Sebastian through the last week?" I draw

Julie toward the wall so that I can have her to myself for a minute. "I think I'm beginning to know how Melissa felt sometimes."

"It's always going to be like this before an opening," she says. "He'll go back to normal after tonight."

"We don't have any normal to go back to. Tomorrow we have the children for a week, and then there's Europe and their summer vacation. I know, I know, I got what I wanted."

"You did want him," Julie says. She smells faintly of lemon.

"No more tea rose?" I see Oliver Remsen trying to break away from a conversation at the bar.

"I'm experimenting, what do you think?"

"I feel like an impostor married to Sebastian; this dress is like a costume."

"Sebastian hasn't changed," Julie says, but Oliver's signet-ringed hand is on her shoulder. I paste on my smile, but I feel a rush of sympathy for Melissa, a woman I always thought it was all right to hurt because she wasn't good enough to Sebastian. She didn't appreciate him, I told myself, as he rolled in my willing arms in the stolen, sunlit moments we had—and so she didn't deserve him. The roar of the party—the sound of connections being made, careers being built and careers crumbling, the thousand subtle interactions which fuel the art world—has reached its crescendo. People are still pouring from the elevator, but a slight undertow has begun to build. It's almost eight o'clock, and I know that Sebastian has started worrying about a dinner he's planned for a few collectors afterward. I turn away from Julie to find him and bump shoulders with Ed Lissner. He leans over to give me a kiss.

"You smell good," he says. Knowing that he's sexual enough to fuck a student somehow changes my image of him.

"Thanks."

"Marriage suits you! You look extremely art-world *grande dame*," he says, standing back a foot and staring at my body in the red dress. "How do you like it?"

"Pretty well; actually it was sort of your fault that I got married at all!"

"Say it isn't so," Ed Lissner says.

"Sebastian was so jealous of your interest in me that day at his gallery that he proposed! So I guess I owe you one."

"My interest! We never even . . ."

"I know, but he picked up on something. Maybe it's because you turned out to be such a big deal." I smile at Ed Lissner, remembering that he's important and rich, wishing he was more attractive to me physically.

"And now you're married, so I can't collect! This is the most depressing conversation I've had all night." Ed Lissner's voice is light, but he seems disturbed. I've probably been too honest with him. I paste my smile back on, and he reaches out and lifts my teased, streaked, blown-dry hair off my shoulder. A finger brushes against my neck. "You're a beautiful girl, Elizabeth," he says.

"The queen welcomes her subject." Oliver Remsen is standing next to me. His face is flushed and he's holding a glass of champagne. "How does it feel to be the Princess of Hype?" He must be drunk, I think.

"Ooooh, nice," Julie says. "Another loyal friend." Oliver turns to her with a gaze like a hungry dog's at mealtime. Men never get angry at Julie.

"Sebastian's created a real feeding frenzy," he says. "There will be a huge profit from this show alone."

"Sebastian needs the money. He's supporting his ex-wife and the children and the gallery. Everything's so expensive!"

"What about George Mallet's children?"

"They made millions and they still sued for more! Sebastian had to settle with them, can you believe that? No matter how much people have, they always want more."

"Somehow I don't think Sebastian's been had." Oliver Remsen eases away through the dwindling crowd toward the elevator.

"He's so bitter!" Julie says.

"He's in love with you, that's why."

"I suppose so. I wish I could just be friends with men, you know, it's the hardest thing for me."

"They worship you!"

"It's not me really, that's the trouble." Julie sounds wistful, as if the emptying room were making her sad. "They obsess about me and think they can't live without me, but if we spend a whole day together, they usually begin to get irritated. They're not really in love with me—they're in love with some fantasy based on me."

"But you never do spend a whole day together."

"Exactly, but how long can I keep that up? They love me as long as they don't have to deal with my messy closets, my checkbook hieroglyphics, my everyday problems with Samantha."

"Do you think *I* fell in love with a fantasy?" My question surprises me, but Julie doesn't seem startled.

"That's one of the dangers with married men," she says. "You don't really know them as long as they're married to someone else. And then when they're not, they're married to you!"

Sebastian is coming toward us. I'm sure that he's going to scold me for not doing my job, for gossiping with my friends all night when I should have been helping him. All those shoulds! I get ready to defend myself.

"You look spectacular," he says to me, kissing my forehead and putting a gently proprietary arm around my red shoulder. There's no criticism; he even seems pleased to see Julie. The show has been a success. The agony is over, until next time. We all smile politely at each other as if everything is fine.

26 "Elizabeth," a quiet voice behind me says. I turn in the marble cloister of the Frick Collection and see Ed Lissner with his dark-haired bimbo clinging to his arm. I've been walking back and forth next to the fountains in a daydream, waiting for Julie, who's supposed to take me shopping across the street at Saint Laurent.

"Oh, hello." I'm glad to see Ed, but irritated by the limpet-like presence of the girl. "This museum is so beautiful," I say. "I always forget how beautiful it is." Ed Lissner nods and the bimbo hums agreement.

"Oh," Ed Lissner says, as if he's forgotten something, "I meant to introduce you. My sister Andrea Lissner, this is Elizabeth Cole, or should I say Elizabeth Smith?"

"Nice to meet you," I say, smiling at Andrea.

"Andrea's here for a week from college and I'm showing her the art-world sights. Sebastian's opening was one of the highlights."

"It was wonderful," Andrea gushes.

"Thank you," I say. "It was certainly a lot of work. I'm just beginning to unwind."

"It must be so *exciting*," Andrea Lissner breathes.

"Yes," I say, "it is." But what I think about is the discomfort of being dressed up like a Madame Alexander doll in a tight red outfit.

"What's *your* excuse for wasting time? I saw you gazing at the fountains; you look just like a kid," Ed Lissner says.

"I'm meeting my friend Julie. We're supposed to go shopping," I say.

"Not going to buy more grown-up ensembles, I hope."

"I don't think they have play clothes at Saint Laurent," I say.

"*Yves* Saint Laurent?" His sister's eyes are wide with amazement.

"The very one," Ed says, in a tone which is both affectionate and dismissive.

"Maybe you'd like to come with us," I say.

"Oh no, in fact I have to run right now. I'm meeting a friend from my dorm at the Whitney Museum!" She makes the Whitney sound like Karnak, or the pyramids. Quickly she kisses Ed goodbye, and leaves us alone next to the splashing fountains.

"You'll have to forgive my sister. She doesn't come to New York very often."

"She's not at all like you," I say.

"Thank God! My mind has been entirely corrupted by knowledge. The rest of my family lives in an easier world."

"What happened to you?" We walk together next to the fountains, wandering through one of the arched doorways into the long gallery where the Turners hang.

"Who knows, I was always different, always reading books or studying while everyone else played baseball. It's such a trite little story, don't you think? They laughed at me then, but of course now . . ."

"But it's *your* story," I say.

"Well, we grew up in a big frame house near Iowa City. My parents wanted us to live a normal life, so there was all this emphasis on sports, dating, the paraphernalia of the typical American childhood. The money came from my mother's father, who had invested in Texas land in the 1930s, but they tried desperately to insulate us from that. The best times I had were when my Uncle Ed came to visit; he lived on a houseboat in Paris and knew a lot of painters, and I was even named after him. As soon as I was old enough I started begging to go to visit him; that's how I ended up first at the Sorbonne and then at Harvard. End of story."

"It sounds more like a beginning," I say. Ed Lissner shrugs

his shoulders, as if to indicate that that's all he's going to tell me right now. He is standing in front of the largest Turner, taking in the vast wash of color and the tiny details of the harbor of Dieppe.

"For me pictures have always been more interesting than people," he says. "Look at this brushwork. Turner was fascinated by the harbors; he took his easel down to the docks along the Thames every day, trying to understand the connection of men and their endeavors to the vastness of the sea, the vastness of nature. His understanding of the anatomy of the water is astonishing. Look at those waves, the way he's painted them actually moving against the pilings here." Ed Lissner directs my gaze with a big gentle hand on the back of my neck. The painting *is* amazing, but I'm much too aware of his hand to concentrate. He slides it down to the small of my back, enjoying the curve of my shoulders. His touch is impersonal somehow, as if I were a statue and he was caressing marble. Out of the corner of my eye I see the disturbance which is my friend Julie coming through the dim light of the entranceway.

"Here comes Julie," I say. Ed Lissner slowly, unhurriedly releases my back. Julie rushes toward us. Her slender body is poured into a narrow black skirt and a camisole top. Her black hair shimmers around her like a cloud. As she approaches us I smell roses.

"Julie, Ed Lissner." I introduce them and Ed holds out his square hand.

"Angel!" Julie turns to me breathlessly, giving Ed a dazzling smile first. "I just *raced* in to tell you I can't shop today. I have to have lunch with one of the doctors, a very important doctor!"

"Okay." I'm disappointed and I wonder what kind of medical man rates high heels and tight black clothes. "I'll call you later if you want, maybe we can do it tomorrow."

"*I'll* call *you*," she says, as if it's me who's breaking our date and she who is the supplicant.

"You look ravishing," I say.

"Thanks. Nice to meet you, Ed." She turns to him with

another killer smile. "I've heard so much about you from everyone!" She leans toward him seductively and the black camisole dips to show more skin.

"Nice to meet you, too." Ed Lissner stares frankly at the view down Julie's clothes. "Are you leaving Elizabeth in my care?"

"Yes, but be careful, she knows how to take care of herself," Julie says, reaching up to tuck a lock of his hair in place as if nothing could be more natural. Ed Lissner blushes. Julie kisses me and rushes out, leaving sexual turbulence and the smell of flowers behind her in the air of the museum.

"She's so beautiful!" I say, pleased with Ed Lissner for responding to Julie's power, and angry with him for the same thing.

"She's quite a come-on artist," he says.

"You didn't seem to mind!"

"She's very pretty, Elizabeth, and I know she's your friend, but from a man's point of view she's much too wild, too crazy. A woman like that is endless trouble."

"Plenty of men are dying for that trouble."

"I'm sure they are, but I've always been a careful fellow. The women who need to give me an erection before they feel comfortable aren't usually the ones I'm attracted to."

"What kind of woman are you attracted to?"

Ed Lissner smiles, but refuses to take my bait. "It depends," he says. "It depends on the circumstances, it depends on the way we meet."

"It sounds like a lot of women, the way you say it." Now I *want* Ed Lissner's admiration, I *wish* he'd put his hand on my back.

"Do you want to have lunch, since Julie stood you up?" he says. "We could just go across the street. I don't have a class till three-thirty."

"Sure," I say, thinking that he's talking about the local coffee shop. Instead, he guides me up to La Goulue and we sit on straw chairs under the awning on the sidewalk.

"I'm a sucker for anything that reminds me of France," he

says. "I go back as often as I can. Let's order the turbot, they make a great sauce here."

I sit back and sip a glass of wine as Ed Lissner orders our lunch in letter-perfect French, which he speaks in his twangy, flat, Midwestern accent. It's a sunny day and the light beams down onto the sidewalk through the vines in front of the houses on the side street. Ed Lissner's attentiveness reminds me of the way Sebastian used to treat me, and I wonder if the freshness of each new relationship, the excitement of the first time you go to bed with someone, the romance of the first lunch, the first weekend is just that—a kind of firstness which is more important than the man himself.

"When do you have time to travel?" I ask. "Isn't the teaching schedule pretty demanding?"

"I was there at Christmas, I'll go back at the end of July," Ed Lissner says.

"This is pretty good." I mix the moist flaky fish with the thick green sauce.

"Everything tastes better in France. I'm taking a bunch of people over there, or at least I'm trying to organize a group in August to visit Lascaux and Les Eyzies and then go down to Vence and the Maeght Foundation. There's still the pottery at Vallauris where Picasso worked, and of course the glassworks and the Léger Museum in Biot. Too bad your husband can't spare you."

"What makes you think that?" Of course he's right, but Ed Lissner's assumption that now that I'm married to Sebastian, Sebastian controls my summer plans goads me toward wanting my freedom back, just the way Ed Lissner's sexual response to Julie made me want him to have a sexual response to me.

"Married is married," he says. "Perhaps that's why I've never done it again."

"It's your fault; he never would have proposed without your attention that day."

"I should think that proposing to a girl like you would be easy."

"Don't you think we've gone beyond that, anyway?" I say.

Ed Lissner's acceptance of my situation bothers me. "I mean, don't you think we've gone beyond the point where you and I could just travel together as friends?"

Ed looks up from his fish and smiles at me. "I think where we are is entirely up to you," he says.

"You have no feelings, no desires?" His passivity makes me aggressive.

"Yes, I have feelings, desires."

"Well, where do *you* want us to be? What do *you* want from our friendship?" I've never had to ask a man this question before. I'm impressed by Ed Lissner's maneuvering, but also uncomfortable. He takes his time answering, while I sit there basking in the afternoon light.

"The truth is, I've never slept with a married woman," he says; his drawl seems broader than ever. "Somehow the idea of doing that offends me. You'll say it's male bonding. I don't know, maybe you're right. You're very attractive, Elizabeth, I'm not saying I'm not turned on. But you're prohibited—at least as I set my prohibitions."

"But what about your *feelings*?" I'm practically begging Ed Lissner for reassurance. Until now, it's been me keeping him waiting, me keeping him at bay. He seems infuriatingly aware of his advantage.

"My feelings don't change, but they don't always control my actions. I told you, I'm a very careful man."

"Would you have slept with me before? I sort of had the impression that . . ." I cut myself off from further desperate questions.

"Would I have slept with you before?" He's savoring his gain, weighing each moment. Leaning back in his chair, Ed Lissner slowly examines my face and then my body with his eyes, moving them up and down stage by stage, as if he is thinking exactly what it would be like to sleep with me. I lean back, too, and spread my legs slightly, letting my skirt fall between them.

"Nice legs," I say. The safety of the situation makes it possible.

"You're playing a game with me," he says.

"Tit for tat," I say.

"What if I said yes, if I said let's go to my house right now? What if I took you up on it? You'd turn me down, right?"

"It was fun while it lasted," I say.

"Bitch," he says. "Do you want some coffee? Some dessert?"

"It's you who announced you're not available," I say. "Coffee."

Ed Lissner laughs. "So I deserved that, is that what you're saying?"

"I have the feeling you're someone who gets what you deserve," I say. "Do you have an erection?"

"Wouldn't you like to know!"

"Just checking," I say, eyeing him over the rim of the coffee cup.

"Why do women need men to reassure them of their sexual power?" Ed Lissner asks. "I've always wondered that."

"Why do men need women?"

"I guess you've got me there." Ed Lissner lapses back into the simple farm-boy manner that I remember from the day I first met him at Ingrid's. It's just as well. I could never cheat on Sebastian, I think. Not after he left his wife and children for me, not after everything we've been through together. I guess that's what marriage is. To get to it you have to tolerate so much that the bonds of shared misery and guilt hold you tighter than any bonds of pleasure. That's what you build a life on. Shared responsibility, shared anxieties, shared problems.

After we finish our coffee and Ed Lissner kisses me goodbye, I wander back over toward Madison Avenue and into Saint Laurent. Mindlessly I flip through the racks of fall clothing already on display in spite of the fact that it's not even summer yet. There are velvets and bright taffetas and gold braid. In the dressing room I strip to my underwear and imagine that it's Ed Lissner seeing my body for the first time instead of myself in the mirror. The minute I slip on a dress, the image is gone. The green silk changes me into the woman who is an appropriate wife for Sebastian Smith, the cool, controlled woman I always wanted to be, the woman I imagined when I imagined marrying Sebastian. But under the layers of green silk there's still that hungry, sexy little girl who would have fucked Ed Lissner this afternoon just for fun if things had been slightly different. I step out of the dress and back into my black linen skirt and white blouse. It's getting late and I still have to shop for dinner. This is the way my life will be from now on, day after day, night after night. Shopping for Sebastian, for the clothes he wants to see me in, getting angry at the butcher because the lamb chops have too much fat on them, taking care of the children, making excuses at work because I don't really need the job anymore, doing ladylike sketches as a hobby so that I'll have something interesting to talk about. On the other hand, I'm safe. Safe from having to come through for men I flirt with. Safe from falling through the economic ice into the ranks of the homeless, the women I see begging at the subway stops, the women who run out of money and have to share their apartments with people they hate or go home and live with Mummy and Daddy. I leave Saint Laurent and walk down Madison, delighting in the feeling of wealth and belonging I have as I look in the windows at the clothes designed for women like me. But I wonder, Does safety always have to be this boring?

I'm about to cross Bleecker Street on my way home when I see an oddly familiar figure walking down the other side of the block. He's tall and stooped, with a long face, and the white-haired woman on his arm keeps pausing to stare into the windows of the coffee shops and boutiques. He walks slowly, stopping with her to read the menu posted in the window of the Village Gate, and although she looks much older than he does, something about her grip on his arm suggests wifeliness. They look like what they are—a suburban couple sightseeing in Greenwich Village. What makes me stop and stare and almost call out is that the man is Dr. Rosen, my psychiatrist.

In his office on the Upper East Side, Dr. Rosen always

seems so handsome. There's authority in what he says, he's usually smart enough to come up with things about me I don't already know. Now, in a moment, I realize that he's just another Bridge and Tunnel Crowd commuter, just another tourist ogling the downtown scene, just another aging schlepper trying to make a living at his chosen profession, just another beaten-down human being. I think of calling his name, or going down the block to accost him, but I don't. Instead, I watch as he shambles on down Bleecker and turns down toward SoHo to see the sights.

27 Just after dawn the telephone begins to ring and jars me out of a dream about sea snakes in the depths of a blue-green lake. One of the snakes had Ed Lissner's face, and Casey was in the dream, too, but it's already forgotten as I open my eyes on the pearly light in our bedroom at the loft. Sebastian rolls over, hands me the telephone receiver, and burrows back under the covers. The black plastic feels cold against my ear.

"Elizabeth." It's a hoarse, choppy version of my mother's voice.

"What's the matter? It's so early." For a moment I think it's still the night Andrew drove up to New Haven after his fight with Julie and that she's calling to say he's been in an accident.

"Your father's apparently had a heart attack."

"Where are you, is he all right?" My voice is shrill. This is the last thing I expected.

"At the hospital. Andrew and Karen are on their way up, I just talked to Andrew."

"Is he all right?" Now I hear an edge of panic in my voice. Sebastian pulls the covers up further over his head.

"He's in Intensive Care," she says.

"Is he all right?"

"Elizabeth"—my mother's voice is tired—"I don't know."

"Oh, Mummy," I wail, but she's not about to be drawn into my ignorant grief. "We'll be there as soon as we can."

"It had to happen sooner or later," my mother says.

"We'll come straight to the hospital," I say. "We'll be there in two hours." I thank God for Sebastian's fast car, garaged a block away. I reach over and push against his shoulder, crying.

"What's the matter?" he mumbles. Maybe if he stays under the covers it will just go away.

"My father's sick!" I'm sobbing now.

Sebastian draws the covers off his face. "What happened?" he asks.

"Heart attack," I sob.

"Oh, poor baby." Sebastian sits up and holds me. I collapse against his chest, letting fear and grief take over.

"Andrew's on his way up there. My mother won't tell me how bad it is, she just won't say that he's all right."

"Don't worry," Sebastian croons, and strokes my back. "We'll go up this afternoon, don't worry, he'll probably be fine." His calming phrases exacerbate my alarm.

"I want to go now," I say.

Sebastian doesn't answer. With a sigh which I take to be impatience at my impatience, he rolls out of bed and walks to the bathroom.

"Are we going?" I call at the closed door; running water drowns out my question. I open the door. Sebastian looks up from brushing his teeth. "Are we going?"

"I guess so," he says. I stumble into the kitchen and pour water into the kettle. The simple domestic act of making coffee is more calming than any words. If I can be here, performing these familiar actions, the grinding of beans, the measuring of grounds, as the morning light streams into the kitchen windows, then the world hasn't come to an end. I get two cups from the cupboard and take the milk out of the refrigerator, letting my panic subside. We'll drink coffee as we have many other mornings, and we'll drive to New Haven, as we have many times, and then we'll see. I watch myself go through the motions of everyday living, as if I weren't there.

It's eight o'clock by the time we start north, and rush-hour traffic, steaming and honking, is lined up three lanes across in the opposite direction. The newsboys at the Triborough tolls wear T-shirts already drenched with sweat, and the sun beating down from the east scorches the pavement. I imagine my father's cool, dimly lit hospital room. I imagine him dead.

I have never seen anyone dead. I never imagined my father could die. He was the constant in my life, the person who would always bail me out if that was necessary—although I made sure it wasn't, just in case he didn't. He was the person who, although he had never taken care of me, *would* take care of me. In order to stop thinking as we pass through Bridgeport and around the curve of the Sound past factories and brick towers, I reach for the radio dial. In the distance off to my right I can see the flat plane of the sea.

I get the Drifters singing "What a Wonderful World It Would Be," and I sing along with them.

"I thought you were upset," Sebastian says. "Is that trashy music going to make you feel better?"

"Yes." I refuse to turn it off, but its power to lift my spirit is gone. I remember with sharp nostalgia all the times I have driven up to New Haven by myself—all the times when my father wasn't sick—in the secondhand Bug I had in college, and the first car I inherited from Andrew, the old Porsche that didn't go over 50 miles an hour, and the Red Menace, Sebastian's unfavorite car. My life comes back in a series of flashes of cars and rock and roll. The Beach Boys hits, "California Girls" and "Little Deuce Coupe" the summer that I drove that Porsche and my boyfriend was a skinny pre-med named David who used condoms, the Elvis revival when the King died and I was going out with Richard, who worked in Andrew's law firm and let me drive his Pontiac Grand Am with the broken muffler. David Bowie's "Let's Dance" from my time with Casey.

Hospital corridors are pale green, with linoleum floors and no windows. A nurse stands at the door of the Intensive Care Unit and then waves us through to a room where about a dozen bodies lie in different stages of dying. My father looks shrunken and powerless, he barely displaces the covers, and green plastic oxygen plugs in his nose distort his features. Behind him a heart-monitoring screen flashes a series of regular beeps showing peaks and valleys as his heart beats. The machine seems more alive than my father, who lies absolutely still.

"Have you talked to the doctor?" I ask Andrew, who is standing at the foot of the bed. The heart monitor's high pinging sound rings above the noises of nurses bustling and soft moans from another part of the room. In the next bed a man lies in a plastic tent while a dark-haired woman sits in a molded plastic chair next to him and weeps.

"Yes. Mom went home for a while," he says.

"Is he all right?" I wonder if my father can hear us speculating on his chances for life and death. He makes no sign.

Andrew nods. "They're not sure, he'll have to live differently, at any rate. Come on outside." In the hall Andrew pours me coffee from a big metal urn. Sebastian goes off to look for a telephone.

"What do they say?"

"The doctor here, Dr. Adams, thinks he'll pull through at the moment. His lungs were filling up with fluid. After dinner last night he just doubled over in pain and Mom called the ambulance. There may be complications, though. This doctor seems to think alcohol had a lot to do with it. He thinks that Daddy may still go through some kind of delirium tremens."

"Alcohol! He's not an alcoholic." My idea of an alcoholic is a dirty, unshaven, middle-aged man panhandling passing cars on the Bowery. My father is elegant, successful, entirely under control.

"I don't know much about it, it turns out," Andrew says. "I guess there are different kinds of alcoholics. He did drink a lot."

"Not *that* much!" Sebastian joins us and pours himself some coffee.

"It looks as if I'm going to have to go back to the city," he says. "Major disasters at the gallery." I nod and give him a kiss. Sebastian's absence or presence seems totally beside the point in this family drama. He holds me close to him, really hugging me for the first time in a long time. I sense his gratitude to me for letting him go. "I'll call you tonight," he says.

Andrew and I spell each other at Daddy's bedside, although there's nothing to do there except watch the pings and ups and downs of the monitor and hold my father's cool, motionless hand.

"He's had a serious heart attack," the doctor says when I finally corner him in the hallway. He's young and gives the impression that he's rushed and tired.

"What do you mean?" I keep pace with him as he moves down the hall. Talking with doctors is always talking in motion.

"Under normal circumstances after an attack like this, we'd administer some relaxants, some tranquillizers to keep the effects of alcohol withdrawal suppressed. We can't do that in this case because of the strain they would place on his heart. We just have to wait and see how the body responds." We've walked down the stairs and through the waiting room to the doctor's office. I can hear telephones ringing and secretaries taking messages through the open door.

"Why not?" I say.

"Two things are happening at once in your father's body. His heart is recovering from an attack, and his system is detoxing. That inhibits our treatment." The doctor taps his foot, he's already told me this in other words.

"What do you mean he's detoxing?"

"His blood work shows large amounts of alcohol, both lobes of his liver are seriously enlarged, his skin shows spider nevi from liver failure, his nervous system is not responsive, he was close to the final stages."

"That's impossible! He was never drunk. I mean, he never fell down or slurred his speech or anything like that." My mind races back through the past, all my memories of Daddy holding a glass or his silver flask, all my never knowing what his mood was going to be, all his distance from the world around him.

The doctor shrugs. "If you'll excuse me," he says, and disappears into the seething demands of his office.

It's late. My father's eyes widen and he struggles to sit up. Good, I think, he's feeling better. It's just before dawn in the coldest time of the night and the light through the windows has lost the heaviness of midnight. The hour of the wolf. He pushes himself upright, pulling the electrode wires attached to his chest dangerously tight.

"Daddy," I say, "relax, you're going to be all right." His eyes stare as if he doesn't know who I am.

"You have to get me out of here," he whispers, straining against the IV cord in his arm and the electrodes. "They're keeping me a prisoner!"

"Calm down, it's going to be fine." I put a hand on his shoulder to restrain him; weakly he slaps at my arm. "Let me go!" he whispers. "Escape! escape!" He pushes off the covers and begins pulling at the heart-monitor wire. I ring for the nurse. My father thinks he's being held in a Russian prison camp. He thinks his family has been brainwashed into keeping him there. In quieter moments he beckons us forward and tells us that there are secret maps and papers hidden in the house which will enable him to escape. He has to deliver them. We must get him out of here. Sometimes he's piloting a small plane across enemy lines, or leading us away from our captors over rugged mountain terrain. When food carts rumble by in the hallways of the hospital, he ducks and pushes us down, too, because he thinks they're enemy tanks. My refusal to help him out of bed infuriates him. "You've never been any help," he whispers angrily at me, his skeletal face strained with fury. "Self-indulgent, selfish child!" I try to remember that he's having the D.T.s. Now even more than at first these scenes have a sharp lack of reality; everything that happens is extremely vivid, but it doesn't really register. It's as if my mind is storing up the experience against a time when I will be strong enough to feel it all. Andrew and I take turns; we eat chocolate bars and drink the rotgut coffee from the big urn and sleep on the green plastic couches in the waiting room.

"She was always fine," Andrew says late one night after he's spoken with Karen on the phone. He unwraps a fresh Heath bar and hands me a piece. "It was me who was the problem." He crumples the wrapper and lobs it toward the wastebasket. It misses, but neither of us has the strength to go to pick it up. My father is asleep, breathing regularly for the first time in two days.

"You were trying out different things," I say, thinking about Julie. "You had to experiment, there's nothing wrong with that, it's part of being young."

"Young and crazy," Andrew says. "What was wrong was the way it made Karen feel."

"Do you think you'll get married?" I expect a snort and a quick denial.

"As soon as this is over," Andrew says instead, indicating the hospital with a weary gesture. "We're going to have a child." It's an unsettling change. Always before when Karen got pregnant Andrew had given an exasperated sigh. "Karen's knocked up again!" he would say, as if it was something she had done on purpose to bug him.

"I hope you're happy for us," Andrew says. I smile and pick up the candy wrapper, dropping it into the overflowing trash basket. Below the thickening ice of our closeness, I can still see the cold dark water of Andrew's unpredictability, his anger at me if I say the wrong thing.

In the morning my father is better. The doctor smiles. My father drinks a protein concoction and calls me Lizzie. His face is gaunt but relaxed. He doesn't remember anything that has happened since he doubled over in pain in the living room three nights earlier. No one tells him. But as I drift off to sleep in a real bed in my parents' house for the first time in three nights, it's Karen whose image floats in my darkening consciousness. I've known all along that Karen was playing it wrong. Now it seems I may have been calling it wrong instead.

I've known all along that you don't entice a man by clinging to him and telling him how much you love him and waiting around as if you had nothing else to do, and always being there when he needs you and being honest about your feelings. Unh-unh! No way! You get a man through deceit. By keeping him off balance. By always letting him know that the next time he calls, you might not answer; the next time he wants you, you might not be there. Men don't like victims, men hate dependence. The more elusive you are, the harder they pursue you. The more you put them off, the more they want you. If you hand over your independence, the whole thing is over! The best way to catch a man is with another man. Sebastian had proposed when he saw that Ed Lissner wanted me. For himself, Ed Lissner wanted me more now that he couldn't have me. That was the way it worked. It had worked with Sebastian and all the other men in my life, starting in college, starting in high school! It had worked with everyone except Casey. Casey was the exception. With Casey I had made a mistake. I thought he would be excited by the rest of my life, by the other men who wanted me, by my reticence. I thought that if I wasn't there when he called me, he would call more often. I thought that by freeing myself from him I would bond him to me. But Casey wasn't turned on by my games the way other men were. Instead, they just made him go away.

28 It's Friday evening by the time I start back for New York, driving the car Sebastian left for me. Four days have passed since the morning when my mother called at dawn, but I feel about a year older. My father's home now, and his frailness has become a kind of testament to what his body endured. He says he'll never drink again. He says he wants to live. His face is thin and fierce, as if he had literally been through some kind of refining fire, or as if he had faced death and stepped aside. As I sweep around the curves of the Merritt Parkway, I think about my father's past. Frames from my childhood slide into my mind like drawings: the time Andrew almost drowned, the time I didn't have a date for New Year's Eve and my father took me dancing, the time I brought a date home from college for the weekend and my father yelled at him for kissing me and the boy never called again, the times his sarcasm sent my mother from the table in tears, the times when she refused to speak to him.

These images could be drawings, I realize, or the beginnings of drawings. Through drawings I deal with the past; that's why those drawings of San Francisco had some power. Drawings reinterpret what really happened, or they insulate you from it so that it's bearable. They're smelted out of the heat of passionate memories, memories which are often so painful that they don't have conscious feelings attached to them. I wish I had thought to draw my father before I left, my father who has resolved to change, even though none of us knew there was anything wrong with the way he was before—or none of us admitted it. Andrew and I brought Daddy home, and Mummy was at her best, waiting for him with lunch on the table and his mail and a light comforter on the couch in case he wanted to sit or felt chilled. They have been married for more than thirty years, and they have begun to look like each other. Both have a kind of proud Yankee stance, and a nose which juts forward to meet whatever may be coming, fair weather or foul. There's a perverse nobility in their marriage which has survived infidelity, poverty, wealth, success, and even what sometimes seemed like a genuine mutual dislike. It may be the nobility of endurance, but it has made them friends. Marcus rushed out to greet my father, Andrew and I helped him out of the car and up the gravel walk, my mother stood waiting at the door.

As I approach the city in the dark, the city and the city's demands begin to reach out for me. In New Haven nothing mattered but my father. Now I remember Sebastian and our trouble with his children and the difficulties before the opening, and I remember Julie and her odd behavior at the Frick and my wild flirtatiousness with Ed Lissner. I also have to finish two more drawings before next week, which is when Sue Stanley wants me to go out to San Francisco for the opening of her group show.

It's after nine when I finally pull the car into the garage, give the keys to the surly attendant, and walk the block back to the loft. Sebastian and I have been talking every day, but just about my father. I remember now that there are a lot of other things we need to discuss. The summer, my work, my apartment, our plans for the children. Why it is that we're not getting along so well? Heavy heat has settled over the city and the streets smell of the day's excesses. I walk quickly, afraid, ducking into the entranceway and checking to make sure no one's behind me before I fumble the key into the downstairs lock. I'm looking forward to seeing Sebastian, my handsome husband. In the loft, the air conditioning hits me with a thrilling blast of cold. Sebastian is sitting off to one side of the door at his desk.

"I expected you for dinner," he says as I walk over to kiss him. A pile of catalogues is propped on the desk next to a bottle of Scotch. He sounds irritated, as if he had something else to do that he could have done if he'd known I was going to be so late.

"I haven't eaten yet," I say. "Do you want to go out? Should I fix us something?" I need a few minutes to get my bearings. The loft looks smaller than I remembered.

"How's it going up there?" Sebastian looks at me now, propped on his elbows, with his hands supporting his chin. I sit down in one of the leather chairs and fill him in on some of the details I've left out of our daily conversations. Dinner can wait. I describe young Dr. Adams and the nurse who has a crush on him, and I make all the painful stories funny. Even my father's delusions become comic in my retelling. Sebastian doesn't laugh. Maybe he knows better. I walk around behind him and hug his shoulders from the back, kissing his hair.

"What's the matter with *you*?" I say.

"Oh, nothing," he says.

"Nothing, as in trouble at work?" I say. "Nothing, as in trouble with the girls?"

"I don't want to bother you," he says. "You've had a hard enough time this week."

"Sebastian! I just got back from New Haven. I'm starving. I need a drink. I have to plan a trip to California I'm probably taking next week. Tell me what's going on. I don't have the time to coax it out of you."

"It's not that important. I know this is a hard time for you. What day do you think you'll go to California?"

"What is it!" I reach out and shake his shoulder. He buries his head in his hands.

"I guess it's better if I tell you," he says.

"Don't prolong the agony, please." I cross the room away from him and reach for the bourbon bottle to pour a drink. I remember my father's drinking and dilute it with a lot of water.

"I'm not sure how it happened, I guess you were gone longer than I thought you would be."

"What *is* it!"

"It's over now, anyway. I'd forgotten how much I care about you, how much this marriage means to me."

"Gabrielle," I say. He nods, still hiding his face.

"Shit!" I throw the glass into the sink, where it shatters and splashes. "Oh shit, Sebastian! I thought you had more class than that. Your gallery assistant—what a cliché!" Sebastian's head sinks lower, until it's resting on the surface of the desk. "I can just hear you now. My wife is away, my wife doesn't understand me. Ugh, spare me the details."

"It's over, at least give me credit for that."

"I'm trying to, but of course you didn't have much choice. How would this conversation be going if it wasn't over?"

"I told her I loved you, that I was staying with you and that this marriage is very important to me. It was just a fling. You're my wife. I belong with you." Sebastian's low voice grates and I hear an echo of the past in his words. Where have I heard this before?

"She doesn't mean anything to me, I don't want this to threaten our marriage," he says, and then I know. These are the same things he said to Melissa every time he ended it with me. These are his lines to his wife—on the occasion of a breakup with his mistress. I'm the wife now.

"You're just a cheater." My anger makes me spit. "You cheat on whoever has the misfortune to trust you, on whoever is stupid enough to marry you. You cheated on Melissa and now you're cheating on me, and if you left me and married Gabrielle, you'd end up cheating on her."

"You have every right to be angry, but I'm begging you to forgive me. It won't happen again." Sebastian's voice comes from his head now buried in folded arms.

"Why the hell should I?"

"Because I want to stay married to you. I don't want another divorce, and because I love you."

"I think you have the order slightly wrong!"

"I love you, that's the main thing." He responds to my fury with obedience.

"What you mean is that you can't afford another divorce!" But my anger is dissipating. What's the point? Sebastian is never going to fight back. He's never going to tell the truth about this. He looks up at me now and his handsome face is seamed by the desk edge. There's nothing to do but forget it and go on. Hundreds of husbands have cheated on their wives, and hundreds of wives have forgotten about it. It's not the end of the world, it's not even the end of the marriage. Everybody does it. Even my parents cheated on each other. It's what you do.

"Okay, then," I say. "But you're going to have to fire her. I can't worry every time you go to work."

"I've already gotten her another job, at Marilyn Ammen's. She left today."

"That's not exactly firing her."

"I'm sorry, but I felt some responsibility toward her," he says. "Do you want me to get you a drink?" He tactfully doesn't mention the drink that's splashed all over the sink.

"God, yes." I collapse into one of the soft leather chairs. The brandy when Sebastian brings it burns all the way down my throat and hits the knots of nerve endings that are clenched at the center of my body. The world takes on a softer aspect. I stop thinking about Gabrielle for a minute and begin to feel sleepy. "That feels wonderful," I say. Sebastian comes around behind me and massages my shoulders, the way I've done for him sometimes. For a moment I think about calling Gabrielle myself to see what she thinks is happening. But what if I caught Sebastian lying? It wouldn't be a complete lie, just a shading of the truth. My muscles relax under his hands.

"I think it's great that you're going to be in a show at Sue Stanley's," he says later. We're both pretending that we're back to normal. "You'll get excited, wait and see, it's a big deal."

"Right now it just seems like another obligation, another thing I have to do."

"It'll be fun, I wish I could go with you." Sebastian's hands are still on my shoulders. He sits next to me in the big chair.

"It's only two days."

"Do you think you'll run into that old number of yours, that Casey guy?"

"I doubt it, he's not much for art." The brandy is making me sleepy and Sebastian's hands seem to soothe aches I didn't know I had. My body is relaxing, my eyes closing.

"I hear he's writing something really poisonous about the art world." Sebastian yawns as if his body, too, is exhausted. "Why don't you have lunch with him and set him straight." Even the idea of lunch with Patrick Casey doesn't threaten the smoothness of my drifting.

"Mmmmm," I say. "Oooh, that's good." I'm home, the week behind me; my father's sickness, my husband's lies, my future all forgotten, rocked into a deep mindless sleep in Sebastian's arms.

29 "Are you all right? I heard about your father." It's Ed Lissner's voice, deep and earnest.

"He's going to be fine," I say, sitting on a stool at the kitchen counter and pouring a cup of coffee from the pot. Sebastian has gone to work, leaving me a love note and fresh croissants. Since I've moved in with him, I'm a lot less compulsive about getting to work on time—or at all. Judith Grimes-Gurewitz has been fired and the office is in disarray. No one seems to notice my absences.

"That can be hard," Ed Lissner murmurs. "I went through a long illness with my father."

"What happened?" I look over at the clock. I promised Julie I'd meet her in an hour to go to an AA meeting.

"Well—" Ed hesitates. "Both my parents are dead now."

"So I hope it's not the same!"

"I didn't mean to suggest . . ."

"There were some surprises," I say. "It turns out my father was an alcoholic and I didn't even know it."

"How did that make you feel?"

"Stupid, I guess. I didn't know what an alcoholic is, maybe I still don't know, and it was right under my nose!"

"It's often the things closest to us that we don't see. I wouldn't punish yourself for that. You know, Elizabeth"—his voice shifts from earnest to husky—"it was nice having lunch with you the other day. Maybe we could do that again sometime, maybe we could plan it instead of waiting until we run into each other."

"I guess I got a little carried away." I remember my spread legs under the table at La Goulue.

"You really turned me on," he says.

"I'm sorry if I was too much of a tease." My prim-married-lady-drinking-her-morning-coffee persona seems incompatible with the wild girl of that afternoon.

"You are *so* sexy when you get going," Ed says. "I've been thinking about you a lot. I wish you *could* come to France with me in August."

"But you don't sleep with married women," I say.

"Elizabeth, I would *love* to fuck you. I've been wanting to ever since that first afternoon when we met at Ingrid's."

"I guess I'm flattered." My own voice has lowered and my body feels hot. No one is immune to lust, not even a young bride serenely sipping her morning coffee. I begin to think about Ed Lissner's hand on my back, Ed Lissner's eyes.

"What are you wearing?"

"Some little lacy nightgown, it's kind of short and frayed," I say. "With nothing on underneath."

"Why don't I just come down there right now?"

"No really, I have to meet Julie soon, I'm just leaving." But Ed Lissner's ardor is contagious. "What would you do if you were here?"

"I'd lift up the nightgown," Ed Lissner says. It's hard to picture his serious, art-scholar manner at the other end of this conversation.

"You aren't at all what I thought you were," I say.

"I always knew *you* were hot," he says. "I waited too long."

"We could still have lunch," I say, remembering all the times I expected Ed Lissner to make a clumsy pass and he didn't.

"How about here, at my house. I could make you lunch."

"Maybe next week," I say, "except I have to go to San Francisco for a couple of days."

"That's right, your show! And here all I can think about is your body."

"I'll let you know what happens, I have to go," I say.

"Where are you going so early?"

"You wouldn't believe it if I told you," I say.

*   *   *

"How often do you do this?" I ask Julie. We're crossing Bleecker Street. My body is still liquid from my sexy conversation with Ed Lissner.

"Every day," she says. She's wearing jeans and a loose T-shirt and she smells again of soap and lemons.

"Jesus. How long do you have to do that?"

"Oh, only today, I mean, I do it one day at a time. It's not so bad."

"How do you have time?"

"I spent a lot of time drinking, getting the booze, getting the drugs. My days are pretty empty."

"Do all alcoholics have to do this?" I wonder if my father will end up going to an AA meeting every day. It seems impossible.

"If they don't want to drink." Julie leads me across Washington Square Park and up toward University Place. As we pass Eighth Street I peer down its leafy sidewalks because I know that's where Ed Lissner is. What would he do if I just appeared at his door after the conversation we had? I wonder if he's there with someone else, if he called someone else after we hung up.

The meeting room where Julie takes me is down ten steps below the street in the run-down basement of a Methodist church. The air is thick with cigarette smoke, and two plates of delicatessen brownies gather flies at the back near a huge coffee urn. Five rows of men and women sit in metal folding chairs, and as we walk in a young woman steps up to a podium at the front. "Hi, I'm Stacy and I'm an alcoholic," she says. Everyone claps as if this is a great thing to be. My eyes take in two scrolls on the wall behind her listing the twelve steps and smaller signs elaborately lettered in old English script with old platitudes. *Easy does it. First things first.* They look like the homilies I used to put on my bulletin board at college, when life seemed very real and very earnest. There are plenty of people in the room with torn clothes and grimy, ravaged faces, but there are others who seem to have wandered in from glossy professional jobs and chic restaurants—of course, no one just wanders into this grungy basement room on a nice summer morning to listen to some drunkalogue. They must be alcoholics. Julie looks like a college kid as she munches on a brownie, but I have a flash of her the day I couldn't wake her up, her deathly paleness and the funny way her body lay under the sheets.

When Stacy's finished telling how she drank her way through life until she was in a car accident, a man who looks like a banker in a well-tailored suit and wing tips passes a basket, and most people put in a dollar or a few quarters. After that people raise their hands and Stacy calls on them. All of them introduce themselves in the same way and the whole room chants a welcome. "*Hi*, Andrea!" they say. It *is* like a bunch of Moonies. Julie was right when she complained that day I visited her at Cushing. The people talk about their troubles and most of them don't even mention drinking. One man's wife has been cheating on him, another wants to cheat on his wife. A young girl is worried about her exams at school. Another woman is having trouble with the willfulness of her teenage daughter. I have a strong desire to raise my hand and talk about Sebastian, but then I remember that I'm not an alcoholic.

After the meeting Julie and I go down to Alfredo's and sit in the tiny graveled garden surrounded by the backs of brownstones. Instead of drinking red wine and picking at her food, Julie spreads butter on one of the warm white rolls and demolishes it.

"I miss you ordering salad and red wine," I say, then wonder if I shouldn't have said this. "You know the doctors are saying that my father's alcoholic."

"That doesn't surprise me," Julie says. "I knew there was some reason why I liked him so much."

"It surprises *me*. I still think of an alcoholic as a grotty panhandler."

"Like me?" Julie grins over her soda water.

"I'm still not sure what I think about you. Am I an alcoholic if I can't imagine going through life without a drink?"

"It depends on how much that desire drives you nuts, or how much it wrecks your life," Julie says. "There's such a thing as an addict with no substance, an alcoholic who just doesn't happen to drink too much . . . yet."

"What would I do without those wild ecstatic moments when I feel as if I'm sailing through everything?"

"Those are the highs," Julie says. "At least you recognize that they're connected with drinking."

"Those first afternoons with Sebastian, the sex and the sunlight, the white wine."

"There are also lows."

"Do you think I should fuck Ed Lissner?" I say.

"Is he alcoholic?"

"No, it's nothing to do with that. He's coming on to me, and he's so aggressive!"

"Why would you want to cheat on Sebastian?" Julie asks. She eats big bites of her broiled fish and vegetable lunch.

"He had an affair with Gabrielle, you know, his ditsy little gallery assistant. I don't know when it started, but it ended while I was up in New Haven taking care of Daddy. Is that tacky? I was furious."

"Oh, Elizabeth." Julie puts down her fork. The news of Sebastian's infidelity seems to upset her more than it upsets me. "What did he say?"

"He said it was over, blah blah blah, that he loved me and that our marriage was very important to him. I let him convince me. I mean, what's the point of making a huge fuss? What good would it do?"

"Is that why you want to fuck Ed Lissner?" Julie asks.

"I don't know, I hadn't thought of that, as revenge, you mean."

"Or to get back your self-esteem, to reassure yourself that you're sexy, too."

"Maybe, although that's not how it feels."

"Lust always feels like lust, no matter what the motives," Julie says. "That's why these things are so tricky. How could Sebastian do that? After everything!"

"He just did. It didn't bother me that much."

"Except that you want to fuck someone else. Ed Lissner's probably responding to your vulnerability, to your hunger. Women send out certain signals when they're available. God-damn Sebastian! Why couldn't he control himself."

"I think it was too hard on him, my being away, and every-one's focus was on Daddy. Sebastian's like a little boy, he needs a lot of attention. When he didn't get it from me, he turned to someone else."

"You're so rational about this! Didn't you just want to kill him when he told you! Weren't you furious?"

"I did throw a glass."

"Well"—Julie seems resigned to my indifference—"at least that's something."

"But not at him," I say.

"If you're going to fuck someone else," Julie says, "why don't you fuck Patrick Casey? He's someone you really care about, you loved being in bed with him before, you're going to be out there, and there wouldn't be a lot of complications. Basically he lives in California."

"It would be pretty complicated if I was still in love with him."

"But you *know* him, you know that he's not the kind of man you could ever marry and settle down with. *He's* the one to have an affair with, if that's what you want to do."

"Is he paying you?" We both laugh. I've barely eaten my spaghetti and Julie twirls some strands onto her plate.

"I have uncomfortable vibes from Ed Lissner," she says, seriously now. "Some men get a little rough."

"So if it's sexy, why not?" I sip my cup of thick double espresso laced with cream and sugar and feel the hit of energy as the combination enters my bloodstream.

"Just tell me that you won't sleep with Ed Lissner before you go to San Francisco," Julie says. "Give yourself some time, you don't know how you're going to feel."

"Okay," I say obediently, "I will not go to bed with Ed Lissner until after I come back from San Francisco." It's only as I say this that I realize I had planned to call him after lunch, that I had planned to spend the rest of the afternoon doing just what he suggested.

"Have you spoken to Casey yet?"

"I don't even know if I want to! Sebastian asked me to call him and talk him out of writing about the art world."

"*Sebastian* asked you to call Casey?"

"Maybe he thinks he can trust me. He's heard that Casey may be doing an article slamming dealers, and he thinks wifely loyalty requires that I do something about it."

"And you think?"

"Casey thinks that *our* friendship requires me to help *him*. Men!"

"You'll decide on the plane," Julie says.

"I'm married to Sebastian."

"That *could* just make it more tempting. Nothing's sexier than knowing you shouldn't, except maybe size."

"*That* makes a difference?"

"Are you kidding?"

"That's not what you read, I mean there are all these articles . . ."

"Come on, the magazines are controlled by men!"

"But with Sebastian . . ." Since our marriage, sex with Sebastian has been rushed and perfunctory. Desire was drowned in a wave of daily concerns. There was always something else on his mind, or my mind. There was no more clearing away afternoon hours for nothing but our mutual physical pleasure.

"Don't tell me anything I shouldn't know." Julie holds up a hand in front of her old, wickedly charming smile. "I want to wish you luck, let's have a glass of wine to celebrate adventure!"

"A glass of wine?" I look at Julie, but her eyes don't seem to register the incredulity on my face.

"Just one won't hurt, it's a special occasion!" And Julie lifts her hand to summon the waiter.

30 The approach to San Francisco International Airport from the air is over salt marshes in a southern, inner pocket of the great bay. As the landing gear creaks and screeches down and the plane descends, the houses and low brown hills of the Peninsula come into focus at eye level. The pilot's going down too soon, too fast, we're going to hit the water, I think. There's a gasp from the man in the next seat who's been reading computer printouts during the entire six-hour flight. Then, at the moment that splashing down seems inevitable, the asphalt runway magically appears beneath us and the lights and towers and the sparse grass at the outer edge of the field. The plane thumps, jolts, and shivers as it bumps off and then finally settles on the ground with a roar of reverse which shakes every bolt and screw. I hoist my carry-on bag from the rack and walk through the big terminal, which looks empty after the crowds at Kennedy. As I step outside onto the covered sidewalk, the warm, fragrant California air caresses my senses. How could I ever have left this place? I hail a car idling at the curb.

"Are you a taxi?" I ask the driver.

"No," he says. "I'm a human being who happens to be driving a taxi for a living." I begin to remember what I didn't like about California.

As the cabby drones on about his unpublished novel and his career as a photographer and his stint at Berkeley and the way Fidel has blown it in Cuba since he, Harry Parker from San Jose, went down there to cut cane in the 1960s, my memories sharpen. The climate in California makes life too easy, too safe. The houses all leak and no one cares because it never rains for long. They're squat and flimsy, missing the excellence of New England houses, with their necessary in-sulated walls and sharp peaked roofs. California is about rec-reation, New York is about creation. Here everyone leaves work early so they can windsurf or jog along the embarcadero; there everyone works late.

The Huntington Hotel is like any luxury hotel in the English Country House manner—these clones exist everywhere in the world except the English countryside. There are bridles and horsewhips on the walls of the bar and hunting prints in the hallways. The difference is the views of the Bay Bridge looping its way across the water past Alcatraz and the brown hills of the East Bay and Oakland on the other side. Out the hall window I can see a slice of twin orange spires cobwebbed together by cables, the Golden Gate Bridge accordioned be-tween the Marin headlands and the entrance to the Bay at Fort Point.

It's still early afternoon when I walk down the steep grade of Grant Street to Sutter and across to the gallery on the second floor of a small brick building. The air is ravishing; palm trees shake in the gentle breeze, and in the distance I can hear foghorns. It seems like a long time ago that I was here in this city with its surprise views of the blue water dotted with sail-boats and its white buildings piled like sugar cubes against the steep green hills.

At the gallery Sue Stanley gives me a frantic greeting, then rushes off to attend to a thousand last-minute details that I know all about. My pictures are grouped in an alcove, facing a wall of paintings from one of the other two artists in the show. These are insipid animal studies by some local Bozo, a canine Keene who draws dogs and puppies with huge, plead-ing eyes. I'm disappointed in the quality of the people I'm showing with, but then I remember Sue Stanley saying that the only reason she could sell my drawings was their subject matter. San Francisco collectors don't like New York artists. My pictures are hung too high, so that the impact of the spaces I've tried to create around the bridge and the hills is lost. I look in the back room and find a gallery assistant named Peter, whom I ask to help me rehang my pictures. He smiles but rolls his eyes as he takes a hammer off the shelf. Artists are soooo difficult. I take a pencil and mark where they should be hung, so that the important spaces are at eye level. Sue Stanley looks over and grimaces when Peter begins hammering, but she doesn't intervene. When Sue Stanley asked to show my drawings I imagined her gallery as sort of a West Coast Gray Anderson; now I see that it's a dinky shoestring operation. None of the pictures is sold before the opening, assistants are on the phone trying to get people to come tonight. For some reason this is exhilarating; I'm as far from my father's world and my husband's world as an artist can be.

By the time I've walked back to the Huntington and taken a shower I'm running late for my own opening. I stand in front of the bathroom door mirror and straighten the black pants and long beige sweater I've decided on. I wonder if Casey will show up. I wonder if he's even in town. He doesn't like drab colors. I take off the pants and sweater and try on the black linen dress that I bought for the opening, too skimpy. Then I try on the black pants with a white silk shirt and a blue blazer, but I look like a schoolgirl. The white skirt I bought paired with the beige sweater makes me look too fat. It's back to the pants with a red linen shirt. I'm still not dressed; I've tried on all my clothes and the show opened fifteen minutes ago. Finally I put on the beige cotton sweater, tuck it into the pants, put the red shirt over it, and tie my hair back with a red scarf. My hair isn't behaving well either. In the mild, dry air it's thick and unruly. When I finally get there, no one notices my entrance. Sue is busy welcoming and wooing, hovering around the animal paintings as if they were the work of a promising genius.

I get a drink of acid white wine from the two jugs on a table near the door and stand as far away from my pictures as possible. Most of the crowd is around the doggy-eyed oils, which have quickly been marked with old-fashioned red SOLD stickers at the bottom, as if this were an antiques show. San Francisco collectors like familiar things. They buy either local art, because it's local, or—when they have money to spend—well-established Eastern artists. They don't take chances. Tonight I seem to be in competition with the other artists, especially with the dog-and-cat man, a bearded overweight aging hippie in thong sandals, who carries a walking stick, wears a red beret, and lives in a houseboat in Sausalito. I don't understand how they can fall for him and his glorified Hallmark pictures. The neatly turned-out San Francisco art lovers and their counterparts, the remnants of the halcyon sixties, ebb and flow in Sue Stanley's two small rooms. The rich women all have bouncy hair and wear designer sportswear; the men wear blue jackets and have the slightly ruddy faces of the privileged class in a provincial city. I drift alone, feeling like some alien, exotic bird, toward the stairs, where a couple of women from Marin County in silk print dresses have paused to let someone up the narrow flight. Suddenly there's a wild commotion, the ladies shriek and step back, a scrabbling snuffling noise comes from the entrance, and a bulldog dragging a red leash bursts through the groomed crowds and heads in my direction.

"Henry, Henry, come back here!" Casey's voice booms from the door. I grab Henry's collar and hold on, kneeling to look up into his master's bright blue eyes.

"Hi," I say. "Why don't you teach your dog some manners?" He looks exactly the same, a completely familiar face in utterly uncomfortable surroundings.

"Elizabeth, how fortuitous!" He reaches over and kisses my cheek. Henry sits on my foot. "What a grand occasion! Which are yours?" I point over toward the wall where my sketches hang, but as Casey moves toward them, he is accosted by one of the printed silk dresses from the stairway.

"Aren't you Patrick Casey? I wanted to tell you how much I liked your piece on the Tenderloin landlords, it was so shocking! You really told them off," and then her Joad of a husband interrupts with his admiration for some other article, and in a minute Casey is surrounded. The other print dress breaks away and attaches herself to me. "I'm Muffy Linkletter"—we shake hands—"and I love your little sketches," she says. I smile a polite thank-you. At least someone has noticed my work! "They're *so* much like your father's work, I'm *such* a fan of his," she says, "and you look just like him! I recognized you from the pictures I've seen of him." My smile loses connection with my feelings, I keep it plastered on as I nod and accede to Muffy Linkletter's praise. Casey looks over at me from the crowd which has cordoned him off with an I'm-sorry-but-I-can't-help-it-if-they-love-me expression. After a few minutes he breaks away and joins me.

"The drawings are really wonderful, Elizabeth," he says. Muffy has miraculously disappeared. "I didn't know that you thought about San Francisco so much, living your glamorous New York life." Casey takes my work as a personal compliment.

"It was a magazine assignment," I say. But before I can tell him how it started with the bad photographs and the cover I wouldn't sign, he's swamped again by the Binkies and Jacks and Theodoras and Dawns, the ones he went to school with and the ones who knew his family and the ones who read his articles—all together this seems like the entire population of the city. When I finally turn to leave and the gallery is almost empty except for Casey and his fans, he leans toward me for a moment.

"Come and have lunch tomorrow," he says. "I want to see you, we can't talk here." He puts a hand on my shoulder. "Please," he says.

"I'm leaving tomorrow night, I didn't even know if you'd be here."

"Do, then. I'll make something you like." He grins in an expression of triumph. He knows no one can resist him—particularly not me.

"I'm supposed to call you anyway. I have a message for you, of sorts," I say.

"I hope it's from you."

"Not exactly," I say. The artist with the red beret and the sandals is rapidly approaching, trailed by a group of his admirers—chattering post-hippie types, the men with graying ponytails and guayaberas or batik shirts, the women with long hair parted in the middle and droopy cotton shifts; a bunch of wilted flower children.

"Good; then you have to come and see me, to tell me!" Casey smiles as if he has single-handedly solved our problem. The groupies are closing in on him, led by their artist idol, probably wanting to discuss New Age religion in art with a real live journalist.

"I'll come about one," I say, and Casey is gone and I'm staring at the back of a woman with a long brown braid and a body odor which is equal parts sweat and marijuana. The Muffys and Harrys have gone out for dinner already, to Ernie's or Trader Vic's, where their wisecracks about outsiders will be chronicled by Herb Caen. The counterculture leftovers will hang around until they've finished the free wine and cheese. I decline Sue Stanley's offer of dinner and walk back uphill to the Huntington. At the top of Nob Hill the sounds of traffic mix with the cable-car bell, the cathedral is silhouetted in the last pink glow of sunset, and far off across the Bay the lights are coming on in other people's houses.

31 I walk too fast up the steps on the back of Telegraph Hill past the gardens below Casey's house. Out of breath, I pause and turn to look at the Ferry Building below me and out at the impossibly blue water where a sailboat race is passing Fisherman's Wharf on the downwind leg with spinnakers flying like an archipelago of bright colors in the sun. I straighten my clothes and comb my hair again, bobbing my head forward to loosen my bangs across my face. Near the sailboats the ferry chugs across the Bay from Tiburon past Angel Island. The gardens, tangled with climbing roses and bright geraniums and impatiens, smell of earth and flowers in the sun. My heart beats too fast, and I will myself to forget the past as I walk the last few steps on the boardwalk. I always imagined that Casey's Irish soul got something out of losing me. He could indulge in a delicious mournful soliloquy, a dramatic renunciation which might be almost as much fun as being together—and a lot less trouble. I pictured him standing up here by his house looking west into the sunset, or drinking down at Gino & Carlo alone and brooding into his whiskey about how he'd lost the only woman he ever loved. It made a good story, and Casey was crazy about stories.

The first sound after the doorbell is a long bark, frantic scuffling against the door, and the scritch-scratching of paws as Henry tries to lift himself up to the window at the side of the entry. Through it I can see polished floor and Casey's front room piled with newspapers, books, and thriving plants.

"Henry!" Casey says in a not at all reproving voice, as he opens the door and the drooling bulldog form jumps up on my carefully chosen pristine little black dress. "I guess he remembers you." Casey leans over to kiss me as Henry leaves a trail of drool across the expensive linen and subsides down my legs, ending by licking my patent-leather sandals. "It's great to see you!" Undeterred by Henry, Casey expands his kiss into a bear hug, pressing me against his chest and stroking my back with his hands. My body responds as I stand there floundering in his embrace. I pull away. I will not allow myself to be swallowed up by Casey's big body and Casey's big mind and Casey's outsized spirit. I have come with a mission.

"I was trying so hard to look great!" I say, standing a safe foot apart from Casey and Henry. "Now look." Casey desists, but Henry proceeds to kiss my legs, leaving a thin layer of slime.

"You *do* look great." He smiles as if he's laughing at my little resolve not to be taken over by his big self. "You haven't changed."

"This is such a terrific house," I say, walking into the front room. Henry has trotted in ahead of me and camped on the sofa where I had planned to sit. I veer toward a canvas sling chair. "You couldn't find a house like this in another city."

"It *is* pretty nice." Casey passes me and walks back to the kitchen, where he opens a bottle of wine and takes two heavy jelly glasses from a shelf. From behind I see that he hasn't changed either, the broad back and the low-slung walk as if he lives in a world where the ceilings are often too low for him. There are a few gray hairs in his long, badly cut, curly hair, which falls to the collar of an old blue-plaid flannel shirt.

"Here," he says, when I'm settled with my glass looking out the window at the Bay, and he hitches up his glass in a toast.

"To the past?" I ask.

"No, anything, but not the past. I'm beginning to hate the past."

"How American of you, how un-Irish." He sits on the sofa next to Henry, with his long legs stretched out in front of him. He's barefoot.

"Maybe I've made some mistakes, that's Irish enough," he says.

"You would have had to move," I say.

"Christ, Elizabeth! You never did learn to beat about the bush. How about a little small talk, a bit of polite banter before we roll out the heavy artillery? You got married, I hear. How is that?"

I shrug. "Do you think you'll ever get married?"

"I would have moved gladly," he says. "What's a house but another place to live?"

"I thought you wanted to make small talk."

"I changed my mind." Casey sips his wine and absent-mindedly scratches Henry's pointed ears. "You look just the same," he says. "It's as if nothing else had ever happened."

"I think I look better!" I want Casey to be impressed by my new polish, the highlights in my expensively cut hair, the luxurious fabric of the drooled-on dress.

"You look the same to me, Elizabeth," and he stares across the room at me as if there is no dress, no intervening space or time. "And you blush the same way," he says, catching my excitement and embarrassment.

"You notice too much!" His smile sends sexual electricity arcing across the gap between us. I wonder if there are other women in his life now. There must be; he wasn't a man who could be without women. There must be other women loving him the way I did—and being loved back.

"It's hard not to notice you, showing up after all this time, looking like you used to look." He shifts on the sofa and puts down his wine. "Do you have time for a little lunch?" he says, and then, lower, "I take it your body is off limits?"

"We can't," I say quickly, before I have time to think about what it would be like after all this time, what it was like.

"And why not?" Casey sits absolutely still, leaning forward toward me.

"I'm married." But I remember that Sebastian slept with someone else when we were married.

"Does that make so much difference? It doesn't make any difference in the way I feel. It's still you; it's still me."

"It *does* make a difference." I'm afraid to go to bed with

Casey, afraid that the power of our connection will sweep everything else before it, all my carefully constructed plans and all my carefully built stability.

"Are you afraid of me?" He's smiling now, as if my fear is infinitely amusing. If Casey has a girlfriend and I do go to bed with him, I wonder how he'll feel about that. I know. He'll feel just fine about it. "It would be so wonderful," he says. "You were always so wonderful to fuck."

"But we're not going to." I look at my watch. In an hour I'm supposed to be back at Sue Stanley's gallery, and then I have to pack and catch a plane. "Anyway, we don't have time." I sit up straighter.

"I love it when you get prissy," he says.

"Are we going to have lunch?"

Casey gets up slowly, but he's made his move and I know that if anything is going to happen now it will have to be initiated by me. I begin to feel disappointed. Casey bustles around making the spinach-and-avocado salad while I drink more wine. Henry thumps off the sofa, goes into the kitchen, stares disgustedly at his empty dish, and then stomps resignedly out to the deck, where he knocks over a large pot of ferns and lies down with a sigh in the dirt. On my way to the bathroom I walk through Casey's big bedroom with more views of the Bay and the sun sparkling down through champagne air. There are books piled everywhere, books about Ireland and books about Nicaragua and books about yeast-free cooking and a pile of battered dictionaries and books of quotations. I find his girlfriend's photograph on a bookcase near the window, a pretty, adoring-looking blonde with long hair blowing around small features. The frame is a cheap silverplate that Casey wouldn't have picked out, so she must have given it to him— but he kept it. I feel unreasonably jealous and very nosy; a search of the bedroom yields no more clues. I'm relieved to find no hair dryer, combs, or diaphragm in the bathroom.

"Lunch is ready," Casey says when I get back. "Where were you, checking out the competition?"

"I don't know what you're talking about!" At this Casey

laughs so hard that I can't help laughing with him. "She looks
pretty," I say. I wish he'd answer with something dismissive,
but instead, he just puts bright red mats and napkins on the
table. The bacon is still warm and the avocado seems to melt
as it hits my mouth, combining its cool sweetness with the
salty meat. "Mmmmm," I say. "Great."

"The right spices, fresh bacon, tarragon wine vinegar." The
only thing Casey was ever pompous about was his cooking.
"Remember how I used to try to cook in your kitchen? What
a hole! You never had any food in that place, just coffee and
an occasional stalk of celery for big moments."

"It's still the same. Sometimes I cook for Sebastian," I say.

"No kidding, the new husband lives with you? I thought he
was such a successful art dealer. Here, try this." He cuts open
a puff of hot bread and holds out a steaming chunk. "It's just
pizza dough, I roll it and bake it fast so it holds the air."

"No, he has his own place," I say. "The bread is good."
The golden crust protects a steaming chewy mass. Casey
doesn't ask any more about my living arrangements. Sitting
there in his house with the cool air blowing through it and
the smell of flowers and eucalyptus, I begin to feel as if we
haven't been apart. We used to do just this, except after lunch
we went to bed. I'm so comfortable that my problems with
Sebastian, my desires and disappointments and the gritty New
York days of my life seem like a distant dream. With a chill
I remember Casey's girlfriend and the chore that brought me
here.

"Damn," I say. "I'm supposed to ask you important questions and now you've got me drunk and mellow and I don't
care about them."

"Poor Elizabeth," he says, passing me a tiny cup of strong
coffee with sweet cream spread in a diaphanous layer on its
surface. "I'm sure your mission was of the utmost importance!"

"This trip had a purpose, and now I don't even have time
for it!" It's time to leave, but I don't leave.

"Drink your coffee."

"It's fine for you to be so calm. You live in this perfect

 house in a city where everyone thinks you're great, and this nice, well, anyway, this handsome dog! It's fine for you!"

"You can come back."

"When?"

"Anytime."

"But I never have time, I'm leaving tonight and I'm never in California, why would I be here?"

Casey just shrugs his shoulders and smiles. He gets up from the table, pulls a sweater off a wooden hat rack, and whistles Henry back into the house. "Come on, Henry," he says. "We'll walk Elizabeth down the hill." The visit is over. Casey stands by the door with Henry on a leash and so I stand up, too.

"What you wanted to do before," I ask. "Do you still want to do that?" Casey drops his sweater on the floor, drops Henry's leash, and takes me in his arms for an answer. Kissing me, he half carries me into the bedroom, and it is just what I was afraid of. Being in bed with Casey again is an explosion of familiar feelings which sweep away everything else, other people, other plans, silly things like plane schedules and appointments. Casey holds my head in his hands as if it were a precious object. When he kisses me, my knees buckle, and then I watch him undressing in the golden light, and he quickly spreads my legs and kneels between them on the bed, and he pushes himself inside me. Oh, he says, oh. Moving back and forth and locked together, flooded with that lovely inner light, it feels as if I'm letting go of everything in the world. I want to fuck you, he says, I want to come inside you, and then he's panting and making crying noises that I hear from very far away, and then we're coming together. A minute later we're lying there, all of a sudden just two people again, side by side on Casey's bed.

"Just another textbook fuck," I say.

"You were always so sentimental, Elizabeth," he says.

It's afterward in the shower that the fight starts. Hot water sluices down over my body, relaxing warmed muscles and loosened nerves. Already my cells in their contentment are forgetting the urgency which made sleeping with Casey the right thing, the necessary thing, something I had to do. It was irresistible, and in his arms nothing else mattered, but now my other life is reasserting itself through the sunlit haze of the afternoon. I'm seriously late. I'll have to hurry to get there before Sue Stanley leaves, and then I'll have to race for the plane. For a moment I imagine not going, calling Sebastian to say I've been held up, spending the night. What would it be like to wake up in the morning here, with him? But then I remember the girlfriend.

"I'm so late!" I towel myself off as I wait for Casey to finish his shower. Casey takes endless showers, he always has time for anything that feels good. First he turns on the water as a kind of signal that he intends to take a shower sometime in the near future. Then while the water heats and fragrant steam fills the house, he talks on the phone or fixes a drink or writes a paragraph or two. Once in the shower he lathers every inch of his body, and at the end he slowly twists the hot-water knob until cool water showers over him. Finally he emerges, pink and water-logged and smelling of the cedar boards which line his shower stall and the minty soap he uses.

"And you've forgotten your mystery mission, Nancy Drew!" he says over the low roar of water. I can see his big body moving behind the steamed-up shower curtain. Beyond him outside his windows the light on the Bay is shifting into the shadows of evening, the islands trail dark scarves in the water.

"It's no big deal," I say. "My husband put me up to it. He's heard that you're writing about the art world and he's afraid you're going to make him look bad."

"That wouldn't be hard." Casey steps out of the shower and wraps a towel around his waist.

"What do you mean by that?"

"Most of the second-market dealers are doing some monkey business, that's why they hate the auction houses now that Consumer Affairs has cracked down on *them*. Frankly, Elizabeth, this started out as a weak lead, but I've been amazed. In the end I was glad that you wouldn't help me—it would have put you in a very uncomfortable position."

"You're wrong. If there was monkey business, I'd know about it."

"You could see it without really knowing about it. Take the Mallet case."

"Sebastian was Mallet's friend."

"That doesn't give him the right to do what he did. Even friends and executors have certain parameters of behavior. The worst thing is that it's all part of a pattern—he's not the only one—a pattern of defrauding both the artist and the collector."

"That's crazy! Sebastian's not dishonest, he'd be too afraid to get caught to do anything like that. Besides, what's in it for him?"

"He's been taking paintings on commission, promising the collector a selling price much less than the painting is worth, and netting a profit plus commission of more than a hundred percent. It's not even unusual! He also bought those Mallet paintings for a ridiculously low price and has now resold at least two of them at a whopping profit—more like *two* hundred percent."

"It wasn't ridiculously low, it was a record high!"

"A record for Mallet as a living artist, but your husband bought them after he died—just after he died, as he was in a unique position to do."

"The kids got plenty of money!"

"That's not the point. The point is, did they get the amount of money that he sold them for, that they were entitled to by law?" Casey slips on his blue shirt and his pants and puts his feet into a pair of battered moccasins. "Did they get the full inheritance left to them by their father, who loved them? The answer to that appears to be no, they didn't."

"And you blame that on Sebastian?"

"Only because it's his fault. That's the least of it! What about that black Stella he sold for George Polker last year, and one this year, too; the Polkers asked for two and five hundred respectively. I tracked down the buyer, who happens to live out here—not an easy thing to do, by the way, just good luck! He paid more than a million for each painting."

"So Sebastian probably gave the extra money to the Polkers."

"Probably. Why don't *you* ask the Polkers? I can't get the great G.P. III to answer phone calls from an obscure radical journalist."

"And you're planning to write this shit? Who'll print it? You don't even have any evidence!" I straighten the expensive little black dress and try to sponge out the spots. I'll have to go straight to the airport. I wanted Casey to see how good I looked and eat his high-principled heart out. Now I'm too angry to care what he thinks. His attack on Sebastian is so petty, so wrong, so obviously motivated by jealousy.

"Evidence is hard to come by, so many people are protecting so many things, but there are some letters about the Stella sales, and there is this collector who's spoken to me."

"You probably stole those letters, or someone did. Does that make you a thief? You're wrong, you're making a fool of yourself. You know, you're so opinionated and often you *are* right, but not this time."

"How nice of you to drop by and tell me that," he says. We're standing at the door. Henry Luce jumps and slobbers, hoping to be taken for a walk.

"I'll call you sometime," I say, "probably when I get back to New York."

"You won't," Casey says, "but I can wait. Someday you will." Then he looks terribly sad. "I'm sorry we ended up quarreling," he says. "You know I still love you. When you've loved someone the way I loved you, it doesn't change, it never goes away."

"But you have another life now," I say, because I don't know what to say.

"Yes, I have a life, and you have a life," Casey says. "Come on, I'll take Henry out and walk you to the garden." We walk in silence, with Casey's arm just resting on my shoulders, and part at the end of the boardwalk. At the bottom of the stairs I look back up and see him still standing there, a large man with a square brindle dog on a leash, motionless in the golden light, watching me leave.

32 Ed Lissner's waiting for me at the corner of University Place. It's a hot day, but he's wearing a light tweed jacket and reading a thick book as he leans against the side of a building.

"Elizabeth!" There's pleasure and a question in his voice. I know he's chosen to have lunch at Randall's, because it's close to his place and he's hoping that we'll end up there after lunch. I suspect that he's arranged to meet me at this corner in the hope that we won't end up having lunch at all.

"Nice to see you." I'm friendly, but I turn definitively toward the restaurant.

"How was the trip, how *was* it having your first show?" Now that he knows seduction has to wait, Ed Lissner is his old friendly Midwestern self.

"It was weird." As I tell Ed about Sue Stanley's gallery, and the droopy dog paintings that are her usual fare, he guides me through the doors of Randall's and we sit in bentwood chairs and order fancy salads and a bottle of wine. "I guess it was disappointing in a way, but I certainly learned a lot. I hadn't realized how pumped up I had gotten," I say. Talking about it brings back my irritation and the unsettled feelings about Casey that were the background music to my two days in San Francisco.

"But it was a show!" Ed Lissner seems determined to be positive. "It was a start. Did you sell anything?"

"Yes. Oh, God." I start to giggle as I remember Sue Stanley's enthusiastic phone call when I got back to New York. "The biggest drawing was sold, but I wish I didn't know who had bought it."

"You do know?"

"Some woman named Muffy Linkletter, who went on and on about how much she admired my father and how much I looked like him! It didn't occur to her that it's not flattering to be told you look like an aging alcoholic!"

"But you sold a drawing!" Ed has lapsed into his old boosterism. There seem to be two Ed Lissners, the raw seductive man of La Goulue and the open-faced cheerleader I'm seeing now. Then it occurs to me that maybe there are two Elizabeth Coles—that part of his doubleness is a reaction to me.

"I guess I shouldn't quibble. Sue got an astonishing price for it, much more than she told me she was asking. I guess she jacked it up at the last minute."

"So being an artist isn't so bad?" Ed chomps away at his lettuce. Green frills protrude from his mouth. He's huge, a friendly dragon just finishing off a young woman in a green dress and smiling about it.

"It's the worst! Haven't you been listening? I hate it as much as I thought I would—more. It's worse for women, too. I get the feeling I'll always be regarded as someone's wife or someone's daughter."

Ed Lissner looks pained. "You have a point about women," he says, "but people will never take you more seriously than you take yourself."

"You sound so patronizing!" Is this the same man who made obscene suggestions to me over the phone? A tiger in bed, a boffo circus bear at the lunch table? "Is that how men always sound, or am I just noticing it?"

"I don't want to be like other men you know. But most men do have different styles for different situations. It's always hard to know how a woman is going to react."

"I apologize, I'm just in a lousy mood because I can't stop thinking about a visit I paid to Casey the day after the opening."

"Patrick Casey? I thought you were never going to see him again." Ed Lissner has finished his salad; he butters a round white roll, takes a bite, and finishes it off. The bread is stale, but he doesn't seem to notice.

"Can you believe Sebastian asked me to call him?"

"From you, I'm beginning to think I can believe anything."
He butters another roll.

"Sebastian heard that Casey was writing something negative about the art world for some mass-circulation magazine. He wanted me to talk him out of it."

"What was it like?" Ed Lissner takes the second buttered roll and dips it in his leftover salad dressing, pressing it around the inside of the empty bowl.

"It was terrible! First, I couldn't help going to bed with him." Ed Lissner frowns and leaves his remaining roll in his salad bowl. "Then we got into a brutal fight. He kept insisting that a lot of art dealers, including Sebastian, are crooks—don't you think there's some kind of personal vendetta there? He said they take paintings on consignment, get the seller to agree to a low price, sell the work for a much higher price, and pocket the difference plus the commission. He also whacked on and on about the Mallet estate, how Sebastian as executor bought paintings from the estate right after he died at that price, knowing that the price would go up, a lot of stuff like that, ugly stuff."

"What do you think?" Ed Lissner's hands are resting on the table; he's sitting completely still.

"I think it's bullshit! If Sebastian sells a painting for more than he expects to, I'm sure he tells the seller—otherwise he'd get caught! He *needs* those collectors, he can't afford to cheat them. As for the Mallet pictures, it was natural for him to buy the paintings he loved when they were available. He paid the right prices." As I speak I realize that I've been thinking about this almost continually since my fight with Casey. These are my best defenses of Sebastian. If Ed Lissner agrees with them, I'll know I'm right.

"Have any paintings been sold since Mallet's death, these paintings Sebastian bought?" Ed Lissner is still motionless. A waiter takes away our plates.

"Yes, I think he sold one to Remsen, and maybe to the Morganthaus or the Polkers, I'm not sure."

"And what do you think he charged them?"

"Well, probably the new price, the one set at that wild contemporary auction, and then his show pushed them up even further. I guess the going price when he sold them." If Sebastian bought those Mallets two years ago and sold them last week, he had made hundreds of thousands of dollars in profit. I wondered where that money went. I knew the Mallet prices had tripled, but my own problems, Sebastian's ambivalence, Grimes-Gurewitz's desire to discover me, and Daddy's sickness had blurred my perceptions of the rest of the world. "I just didn't think about what Sebastian's profit was," I say. "It was right in front of me and I didn't see it. No wonder the Mallet children were unhappy."

"And what about commissions?" Ed Lissner takes a deep breath as if he's entering a cave or diving into icy water. "Do you remember what the Polkers wanted for that black Stella?"

"I overheard G.P. III say half a million, I'm not sure."

"Do you know what Sebastian got for it?"

"Casey claims he found the buyer, that whoever it was paid more than a million. I didn't tell him this, but I think I heard Sebastian say something like that to one of the assistants; I wasn't really listening. Anyway, how do we know the Polkers didn't get the extra profit? I'll ask Sebastian."

"I'd ask the Polkers if you really want to know." Ed Lissner is straining toward me across the table. He looks exhausted. A waiter brings us coffee and he quickly gulps down half a cup.

"Oh, come on, what's wrong with it anyway if he *did*? If he's smart enough to bring it off?"

"It's illegal. He could get the entire profession investigated by the Department of Consumer Affairs, he could go to jail. It's theft, Elizabeth. He didn't buy the painting from the Polkers and resell it, he didn't take that risk. If he had gotten a lower price, they would have lost. They owned it. It was sold. They didn't get the money it brought, it's that simple."

"So you agree with Casey."

"Yes."

"You knew this stuff all along. You knew Sebastian was

doing this, why didn't you tell me? You knew I was going to marry him!"

"You didn't ask, Elizabeth."

"You didn't think I'd be interested? You didn't think I ought to know?" There's the difference between Ed and Casey, I think, between the rest of the world and Casey.

"You're very upset about this," Ed Lissner says.

Suddenly I realize something else that's been right in front of me for a long, long time. I love Patrick Casey. I've always loved him. There was never a time when I stopped loving him, in spite of everything that happened. Casey is the man I belong with. I smile at Ed Lissner. He's the man who somehow made me understand that I have always loved Casey, so I can't help loving him a little.

"Don't do anything rash," he says. "I'd wait and see how much of what you suspect is really true."

"Oh, it's true, all right. You know, Ed, you've been a wonderful friend to me," I say. "I wouldn't want to do anything to jeopardize our friendship." Thank God, I didn't sleep with him.

At this, Ed Lissner bursts out laughing. "Spare me! spare me those old clichés," he says. "If you don't want to sleep with me anymore, just say so."

Now I laugh. "It's not that you're not attractive," I say.

"I asked you to spare me! Shall I walk you home? Isn't there some big art-world do tonight? Even I got invited."

"Are you coming?"

"I never go to those things, too much politics, too much intensely boring conversation. Sebastian's job isn't so easy; he has to be nice to all kinds of real jerks. Maybe he deserves whatever he can get."

"Ed, let's drop it." We're standing outside the restaurant now.

"Do you want me to walk you home?"

"That's okay; I have some things to think about," I say, and I give Ed a kiss on the cheek.

"You can tell Casey he owes me one," Ed Lissner says.

33   "You look pretty sexy in that black underwear," Sebastian says. His dress shirt drapes over his blue oxford boxer shorts as he buttons silk suspenders onto the trousers of his evening clothes.

"Thanks." I pull up sheer black stockings and attach them to the delicate garters of my best Merry Widow. The lace smells slightly of sandalwood and roses from the sachets Sebastian's maid puts in the drawers. The dress lies ready on the bed. Tonight we are going to a black-tie dinner in the arched Blumenthal Patio at the Metropolitan, given by the president of the museum for a new paintings curator. It's the kind of party I imagined we would go to when I was Sebastian's mistress. "This is a great dress, thanks for making me buy it."

I had thought the dress was too expensive—all those layers of lace—and too flashy—all that bare shoulder—but when I had described it, Sebastian had slipped a wad of hundred-dollar bills in my purse and sent me back for it.

"Why don't you come over here for a minute before I put my pants on," he says.

"Oh, Sebastian, I can't. I mean, I'd have to take the stockings off and these panties are under them and . . . why didn't you think of this before?"

"Why don't you let me deal with those panties?" he says.

"And my hair, they spent so much time this afternoon getting it right. Let's wait until afterward, please."

"Spoken like a true wife," he says, pulling on his pants and opening his leather stud box. I hope he isn't going to ask if I talked to Casey when I was in San Francisco. That seems like a year ago, anyway. I just want to go out for dinner in a formal setting where everything's in order and make polite small talk and forget. Just for one night.

"When you were in California, did you have a chance to call what's-his-name?" Sebastian asks.

"Those are beautiful studs," I say. "Weren't they your father's?"

"My grandfather's," he corrects me. "You know, that Matt or Jack or whatever his name is."

"I did talk to him. Do you think my hair looks too stiff like this? To get this much volume he had to use gel, so it's not so shiny." All I want is a few mindless hours. For just a few hours I want to be a puppet, the ornamental wife of the well-born, well-dressed, well-respected Sebastian Smith. One last time. Casey probably doesn't own an evening jacket. Henry Luce would have slobbered on it, anyway.

"Did you set him straight?" Sebastian threads the studs into his dress shirt and loops a black silk bow tie around his neck.

"Not exactly. What time does the invitation say?"

"Well, Elizabeth Smith"—Sebastian wheels on me, completely and flawlessly dressed. I'm still sitting on the edge of the bed in my underwear—"*did* you do something about it or *didn't* you do something about it?"

"I did something about it." I sit frozen on the bed next to my dress.

"And what, may I ask, did you do?"

"I talked to him about it, Sebastian. I defended you. But I couldn't ask him not to write something that's true; I mean, he wouldn't listen to me." That was one of the things I had wanted to say to Casey when I called him this afternoon after my lunch with Ed Lissner. One of the things. He wasn't at home. I left messages at all the usual places.

"What am I to take it you mean by that confused statement?" Sebastian leans against the elegant molding along the door frame, which sets off the luxuriously simple lines of his clothes. He looks slim and what-the-hell and a little bit drunk, like a character in a Fitzgerald story.

"He's right about the Mallet paintings; you did buy in and

then make a huge profit, and I'm not sure, but I also think you cheat on commissions."

"Cheat is not a friendly word, Elizabeth. As for the Mallets, as you know, I bought them at the price of record, market value."

"But that was the price before he died, you knew there would be a huge profit, you had that show to drive the prices up!"

"And if I don't make a profit, my dear Elizabeth, who do you think will buy you evening dresses and take you to parties?"

"That's not the point! You bought them in, and another thing, you sold that black Stella of the Polkers for a million two, right? Did you pass the profit on to them?"

"I gave them the price they had agreed to minus my twenty percent commission. They got what they asked for; they were very pleased. What's the matter with that?"

"But *they* didn't know what *you* got!"

"They're paying for my expertise; what I got, who I sold to, these are things no dealer will tell and no collector asks. I took a gamble and won."

"But there was no risk! It wasn't a gamble! If you'd gotten less, they would have gotten less; since you got more, they should have shared in it."

"That guy has certainly been feeding you shit!" Sebastian's face is flushed. "Buying and reselling is what art dealers do. That's how I make a living, don't pretend you didn't know that! As for the Mallets, those children are millionaires, thanks to me!"

"Then why did they sue you?" I slump down. I wish I could put my head on the pillow and sleep. I don't want to fight with Sebastian. I didn't want to fight with Casey.

"Christ, Elizabeth, people get sued all the time. I thought you were on my side! A wife is supposed to support her husband, not believe anything bad that anyone says about him."

"I *wanted* to be on your side."

"I'm certainly not the worst of the second-market dealers— I'm just one of the most successful. A lot of what you're hearing is jealousy."

"That's what *I* thought."

"Everybody does this, it's common practice. If the collectors don't know, it's because they don't want to know. What's the problem?"

"I guess the problem is me," I say. " 'Everybody does it' sounds good, I know. It's just not good enough." Everybody does it, that's how I had justified abortion, and adultery, and Julie's addiction, and my father's drinking. There was nothing really wrong with these things because everybody did them.

That's what I thought.

"You're a fine one to pass moral judgment: you've done your share of cheating!"

"You're right. I just can't help it, I guess I've changed my mind."

"Is this some kind of punishment for that little fling with Gabrielle?"

"Gabrielle?"

"Because if it is, this is very, very unwise of you. Women are incredible!" Sebastian explodes, his hands gesture. The crystal-and-gold cuff links and studs flash. "They never forget, it's just what they say! 'Hell hath no fury like a woman scorned.' "

"It's nothing to do with that."

"I *bet*!" Sebastian says. He's found his own solution to my problems. "We're late, why don't you finish getting dressed?"

"I think I'll skip this one." Suddenly I know that I won't be going to the glamorous dinner in my wonderful dress, and that I won't be eating médaillons and morels and chatting with important people about their contemporary collections in the Blumenthal Patio tonight.

"Don't be stupid, we'll get over this. It's a seated dinner; everyone will notice if you're not there."

"I'm not going."

"All right, have it your way," Sebastian says. Casey had said the same thing, hadn't he? I wondered if he would call me back.

"I don't want to be late, if that doesn't offend your new extra-pure sensibility." Sebastian moves toward the door.

"Okay, enjoy it," I say.

"If you change your mind, we probably won't sit down until nine o'clock. And when you leave, don't forget to write a note to Dora to make up the children's beds," he says. "They're coming for the weekend."

"Sebastian?"

He turns toward me from the doorway.

"Why don't you go fuck yourself."

34 There's a pile of mail resting against the inside downstairs door to my building when I get home. A postcard from Julie, who's touring the châteaux of Burgundy with a French count she met at a Memorial Day bash in East Hampton. A wedding invitation from Andrew and Karen. Karen has written a row of hugs and kisses across the top. It's late, the rooms are dark, but so familiar that I almost don't have to turn on the lights. I've left all my new Italian silk nightgowns at Sebastian's, so I fish an old cotton nightgown out of my drawer and curl up in bed, calm and exhausted. The smell of the soft blue cotton makes me feel younger, and the city outside seems oddly still. A cool breeze blows summer in through the screens, and I fall asleep to the familiar sounds of the leaves rustling and the distant horns and low roar of the traffic on Houston Street.

"This is all happening very fast," Dr. Rosen says the next morning.

"I saw you on the street the other day," I say.

"What did that mean to you?"

"You didn't look the way you do in here at all. You were with a woman." I don't want to say that he was with an old woman.

"And who did you think that was?"

"Maybe your mother?" At this Dr. Rosen smiles. Back in his leather chair with the Japanese prints on the walls and the important-looking papers on his desk, he has again become a figure of authority.

"It *was* you, wasn't it, walking down Bleecker Street?" The man in front of me looks so unlike the man I saw that I begin to doubt myself.

"If it was"—Dr. Rosen leans back and makes a steeple of his fingers—"what does that mean?"

"You're nothing but an old man," I say. "You looked like just another stupid tourist."

"And how can someone help you if they are just another human being, is that it?"

I bow my head. "I guess so. It seems as if everything is changing all at once. Is that how things happen?" With my head down I feel tears. Why do all these revelations have to pile in on top of each other?

"Sometimes." Dr. Rosen stretches his feet out on the hassock. "Now tell me more about Casey," he says.

"I'm beginning to feel that I can't catch up with my own life," I say, "that the whole thing is slipping out of control."

"Do you need to control everything?"

"I like to, I'm more comfortable that way. One of the things about Casey was that I never could control him. I don't know if I can live with that, I really don't know. It's just that I've realized that I've always been in love with him. That's why he made me so angry! It never changed."

"You're very vulnerable right now."

"I feel vulnerable, but like something just born, like a colt that doesn't have its legs yet. All my life I've been trying to be normal, trying to be like other people, thinking that 'everybody does it' is a sufficient creed. I've changed. I didn't mean to, but it happened."

"Have you talked to Casey?"

"No, but he left a message for me. He's going to be in New York this evening; there's some story he has to do."

"It couldn't be you?" Dr. Rosen asks.

"It will be me," I say. "But listen, he's just part of it. It's because I've changed that I can go back to him—if he still wants me. I understand now that he is the way he is and that's not going to be any different. That's good enough."

"Don't you feel some sense of failure about your marriage? That it didn't work?"

"I know I should, but it seems so clear now. I married Sebastian because I needed protection. I was willing to put up with anything, to overlook anything! I think I had to live through those fantasies to grow out of them." Behind Dr. Rosen the summer heat steams off cement back lots, and the sun glints off the aerials and chimneys of the Upper East Side.

"Is that what you think?" Dr. Rosen swings his chair around. He actually smiles at me.

35 As I turn onto Twenty-third Street, a man in
a tattered, flowered housedress rattles a can at
the corner, and an impeccable couple in white
linen hail a cab going toward Fifth Avenue. I walk past the
big windows of the carpet and furniture warehouses, dodging
boxes and dollies loaded with the last delivery of the day. Casey
should be arriving at the Chelsea about now. I try to speed up
my walk, but the humidity makes a virtue out of rambling.
Ahead of me I can see the wild cast-iron balconies and brick
gables of the big hotel where Casey always stays because it's
the only one in New York that lets him bring Henry. The
lobby is empty. When I ask for Casey at the desk, a frowsy
room clerk with two days' growth of beard hands me a room
key and a folded note.

Wait for me, the note says in Casey's erratic, large script.
I'll be back before six. I look up at the clock over the clerk's
head. It's six-fifteen. I take the tiny, creaky elevator up to the
fourth floor; as I put the key into the lock, I hear an anxious
scrabbling on the other side of the big wooden door. Henry
jumps up on me before I'm into the room, landing big wet
kisses of welcome on my freshly ironed cotton shirt and jeans.
At first I resist him, thinking of how much better I'll look when
Casey gets back without dog drool all over my clothes, but
then I relent. Henry and I will wait for Casey together. I sit
on the huge battered sofa in the high-ceilinged room with the
summer evening light streaming through weathered French
doors, and Henry clambers gladly up next to me. After a
moment he rests his velvety jowls on my thigh with a grunt

of contentment. I reach over and pat him, putting my arm around his big, square head, and he settles himself deeper into the cushions with another grunt. I think about the morning that Marcus Garvey stole Sebastian's loafer, and I laugh.